'Mesmerising.'

Trish Jackson, Author

☆ ☆ ☆ ☆ ☆

'This fast-paced novel draws you effortlessly into the shocking lives of the characters and leaves you feeling bruised by their experiences. The courage of the main character makes this a book full of hope.'

Cath Rundle, Reader

☆ ☆ ☆ ☆ ☆

'An intense reading experience of an immensely tragic story, with a bittersweet ending. An unusual and outstanding thriller, too real to be fiction.'

Derek Hall, Reader

☆ ☆ ☆ ☆ ☆

GUILT

Joan Ellis

First published in 2014

Joan Ellis Publications
Dream Cottage, Main Road, Brighstone
Isle of Wight
England   PO30 4AQ

www.joan-ellis.com

'GUILT' First Edition
by Joan Ellis
ISBN 978-0-9930091-2-9

Cover design : Chee Lau, Sophie Boyes
Typesetting : The Artful Bookman
Printed in Great Britain by imprintDigital.com

For my Dad,
always in my thoughts

You died in April 1965, a month before your fifth birthday. You were probably dead long before Mum downed her third gin with Porky Rawlings.

Just before she left the house, we hid her keys. When she realised they were missing, she got angry and started shouting at me, saying she would tell Dad when he got home. The threat worked. You retrieved the keys from behind the cushion and I tried to say sorry by giving her a kiss but she turned away to hug you instead. Then she took two of her yellow 'sweets', the ones she kept in the cupboard over the sink.

'Promise not to tell Daddy?' she asked when she caught me watching her. 'Here, have a biscuit.' She held the tin open for me. She was smiling. I remember the specks of red lipstick on her teeth but her eyes were hard like pebbles. Tentatively, I reached out. I was never sure with Mum. She was just as likely to slam the lid shut on my hand, as she was to give me a treat. With her bright blonde hair and blue eyes, I thought she was beautiful. On the rare occasions she smiled at me I would have agreed to anything. But she wasn't smiling; she was looking at me in that way of hers. The way I didn't like. The way that made me click my tongue against the roof of my mouth.

'Hurry up,' she hissed. 'And stop making that bloody noise.'

1

I couldn't help but click again. Click, click, click. That was it. She reared up, her eyes wide and threw a handful of biscuits at me. The corner of a custard cream caught me just below my right eye. I never knew a biscuit could hurt so much. I let out a gasp as I brought my hand up to my face.

'Ungrateful madam,' she said, throwing the tin down, causing the biscuits to jump onto the floor, where they crumbled. As she stalked out of the room, I spotted you through the banisters, sitting on the stairs, your fingers in your ears.

'I can see you,' she said speaking to your reflection in the hall mirror. 'Mummy's good boy, aren't you?'

Taking out her lipstick, she winked at you before renewing her special going-out smile. She pursed her lips together as she tweaked her curls, rearranging them to frame her face. I watched fascinated, as she sucked in her stomach, turning from side to side, admiring herself in her red dress, its clingy fabric accentuating the roundness of her hips.

'What you looking at?' I knew better than to answer back. 'Give Mummy a kiss, Mark.'

She offered you her cheek. As she stood on the first stair and bent over, her dress rode up to reveal her suspenders and the top of her white thighs. Standing there in my tartan trousers and thick woolly jumper, I remember thinking how cold she must be. She gathered you up in her arms, planting a Cupid's Bow smudge on your forehead. When she saw what she'd done, she took out your hanky, the one with the letter 'M' embroidered in blue on the corner, then told you to spit on it before rubbing it gently against your skin.

'That's better,' she said, stuffing the hanky back up your sleeve.

She sat on the stairs and settled you on her lap as she hugged you to her. I longed to feel her arms around me. My insides knotted together. I know you never meant to, but you came between us. If you hadn't been there, she would have had no choice but to cuddle me. When you were first born, Mum and Dad made such a fuss of you, I wanted to put you in the bin. It seemed my parents only had so much love to give.

'I'm off,' she said opening the front door. 'You're in charge. Look after him.'

I was seven years old.

I clicked my tongue against the roof of my mouth again. Luckily, she didn't hear, she'd already left. As soon as the door closed behind her you shut your eyes and put your fingers in your ears just like you always did. I sat beside you, my arm around you, trying to comfort you.

Suddenly, you leapt up and ran into the kitchen. I followed and watched as you dragged a stool over to the sink, climbed up, turned on the taps and got a glass of water. Then, you reached up and opened the cupboard.

'Don't, Mark,' I said as you grabbed Mum's bottle of 'sweets', but you weren't used to doing as you were told. She let you do whatever you wanted. Besides, you were too busy to listen to me. When you couldn't unscrew the lid, you wrapped a tea-towel round it just like you had seen her do countless times before. I'll never forget the look of triumph on your face when you finally got the top off.

'Mum will be angry,' I warned.

'Don't tell. Cross your heart and hope to die,' you said. You were concentrating hard on removing the cotton wool stopper and tipping the pills into your hand. Too many for you to hold, you dropped some and watched as they skittered across the floor.

'Damn!'

'Ssch! That's a bad word, Mark.'

'Daddy says it,' you replied, showing me your treasure. The sweets looked lemony, like they might taste of sherbet. Where was the harm? After all, Mum took them all the time and she was fine, sort of. Perhaps she said they'd make you ill because she wanted to keep them all for herself. I reached out to take one, my fingertips just brushing the smooth surface.

'Dare you, Susan.'

'No,' I told you, standing back, knowing how cross Mum would be when she found out. 'I'm not playing.'

I'd like to tell you what happened next but I can't, Mark. Whatever it was, is hidden, masked by too many memories. It's the reason I'm talking to you; I need you to help me discover what went on.

As I waited for Dad to come home, the only sound was the ticking of the clock, its black hands unstoppable, moving unstintingly around its hard, miserable face. I will never forget the exact moment he got home. The little hand was on the eight and the big hand just past the nine when I heard his key in the lock. Then I saw his face, which was one enormous gaping mouth when he spotted you on the floor and me curled up next to you, like a dog.

'Mark's asleep and he won't wake up.'

'What happened?' he yelled from the hole in his face.

I wanted to tell him, I really did but the words were stuck. I pointed to Mum's 'sweets' scattered across the scratched Linoleum like yellow polka dots. Fists clenched into weapons, eyes wild, Dad stood in the doorway, staring down at you. I had seen him angry many times but never like this. He ran over to you, looked like he was going to kneel down but then walked away. He paced the room, his eyes on you the whole time. I started crying, begging him to do something to wake you up. 'Shut-up!' he cried dashing into the hall. I thought he was phoning for help but I didn't hear him speak to anyone. After what felt like forever, he came back and flung himself down beside you, forcing his fingers into your mouth. When he brought them out they were covered in slime. He wiped the stuff on his trousers, then pinched your tiny nose between his thumb and forefinger and put his mouth over yours, like he was about to give you a kiss. You still didn't wake up and I watched in horror as he placed his massive hands on you, completely covering your chest, pushing down gently at first but when you didn't open your eyes, pumping harder and harder, faster and faster.

'Don't!' I screamed running over to try to pull him off you. 'You'll hurt him.'

He swatted me away and put his ear to your chest. Nothing. Silence. More silence than I had ever heard. Then our house filled with the sound of your name as Dad shouted it over and over until it didn't sound like 'Mark' anymore just a terrible noise. You wouldn't have liked it. You would have closed your eyes and put your hands over your ears. Dad went quiet and for a second I thought you must have opened your eyes but then he began to howl like next-door's dog when it was shut out in the garden all night. Hearing him cry was even more frightening than seeing you lying there. At least you were peaceful. Dad wasn't being Dad. He was on the floor, knotted into a ball, his fist forced into his mouth as far as it would go.

'Mark! Wake up!' I urged, terrified, kneeling down and gripping your hand.

I didn't like the way you felt, all cold. I gave your hand a squeeze to encourage you to do the same back. I kissed your forehead, whispered your name. Nothing. You looked peaceful, like you were asleep but you weren't breathing. Even I could see that.

'Please, Daddy, help Mark. Please.'

Back then, I was young enough to believe Dad could do anything. He had always been your hero. You were both so alike. With your dark hair and brown eyes, you were a Wheeler through and through, unlike me with my freckled skin and fair hair.

When Dad tried to get to his feet, his legs buckled. After a couple more attempts, he stood up and set off unsteadily, hanging onto the furniture for support as he stumbled back into the hall towards the telephone.

'Ambulance,' I heard him say.

I had never heard him speak so softly. It frightened me more than all his shouting. He was talking so slowly he sounded like one of his records when he accidentally played it at the wrong speed.

Mum arrived just before the ambulance. I will never forget her face when she saw you. Collapsing on the floor beside you, her tears coloured by mascara, like black diamonds falling into your hair.

'It's too late,' Dad told her.

He was still angry; I could see that. His words hung like lifeless flies in a spider's web. I understood what he meant. You had gone and I would never see you again, like when Dennis-from-across-the-road died from an asthma attack and after that, there were never enough kids in our gang to play Cowboys and Indians. But you weren't Dennis. You weren't dead. You couldn't be. You were my brother. Perhaps it was just one of the many things Dad said to Mum to upset her.

'You killed him,' said Dad grabbing her by the arm and hauling her up. Her knees buckled but he yanked her about like a puppet on a string, revealing her laddered stockings and coat buttoned up all wrong. What had happened? She had left the house looking perfect.

'You killed him,' he repeated, letting her drop to the floor as he picked up the empty pill bottle and hurled it across the room. 'You and your bloody tablets.'

To my surprise, the brown glass bottle didn't break but ricocheted off the wall and skimmed the floor, until it eventually struck the skirting board and stopped. Mum melted down the wall, clawing the wallpaper with her painted fingernails.

'I loved him,' she insisted as if the feeling belonged to her alone.

'You loved men more,' he replied, sounding just like Dad again. 'You left two kids alone in the house. What were you thinking?'

Somehow, Mum managed to get to her feet, her body swaying, her eyelids flickering. I thought she might faint but instead she stood there and threw up over her shiny shoes. It splashed up her legs and stank like sour perfume. Luckily, it missed you. Mum wiped her mouth on her coat sleeve.

'No...Mark, not my Mark!'

Dad slapped her. Her hand flew to her cheek. Then, she flew at him.

'Stop!' I shouted running between them.

'This is your fault, you were supposed to be looking after him,' Mum told me, her face red and running with black tears.

'Mummy, I didn't mean...' but before I could finish, she opened her mouth and roared. Her breath smelt of sick and her body gave off a horrible musky odour. I didn't like it and ducked into the hallway just as the bell rang. Suddenly our box of a council house filled with strangers, all swarming around you, asking Mum and Dad questions, writing things down. One man even took photographs. All those people were there for you but not one of them noticed me. A man with no hair was talking to Dad, and Mum was telling anyone in a uniform she had just popped out and had only been gone five minutes. Dad opened his mouth to say something but she grabbed his hand.

'Please, don't. No more pills, no more drink, I promise,' she whispered.

'That's two out of three of your vices,' he hissed. 'I told you and I'll tell them; you killed him. You and your bloody tablets.'

'I only take them because of you.'

The Man with No Hair looked at them and scribbled something down.

'Shut up, you mad cow,' said Dad, licking his lips.

Confused, I ran from one to the other but I was invisible, dead to them. A lady in black swooped in and grabbed me. I pulled away but The Crow Woman gripped me in her talons, her face twisted into a smile that was not a real smile. Then the Man with No Hair spoke and everyone listened. Even Dad paid attention but I could see he hated it. For once, I agreed with him; I wanted everyone to go away. The only person I wanted was you. Once the man stopped talking, everyone started shouting at one another again. Why? Even I knew words would not wake you.

It was odd. All these people were there because you weren't. I was alone. No more Mark. No more eating biscuits together in bed, in secret. No more sneaking into Mum and Dad's bedroom, taking out her roll-on flesh-coloured corset and sniffing its rubbery smell. No more coming second to you. Now, it was my turn to feel sick. My tummy ached but this time I knew the pain would never go away.

Dad was shouting and Mum was crying all over you. The Crow tugged at my arm and her pretend smile disappeared. The room went quiet. I looked round. You had disappeared. I screamed. Mum ran out of the room, crying for her baby. Hands reached out to grab her. Dad said nothing. Someone picked up the empty pill bottle and showed it to the Man with No Hair before dropping it into a clear plastic bag. Everyone was making a big deal about a small bottle. The same bottle you had watched Mum open every day.

'Markie, get Mummy a drink,' she would ask, tipping two of the yellow sweets into her palm, before popping them into her mouth.

Like a good boy you did as she said, dragging the stool to the sink and clambering on, before filling a glass with water from the tap.

'Clever boy,' she would say, taking the tumbler from you and gulping back the water. 'These are Mummy's sweets, not Mark's... not for little boys. You mustn't eat them. Don't want you getting ill, do we? Promise? Cross your heart and hope to die?'

9

You would nod obediently. Then she would take your hand and draw your finger across your chest in a criss-cross motion. It must have tickled because it always made you laugh.

But that day, you broke your promise.

And that's why I'm talking to you now because I need to understand what really happened. Was it my fault? Could I have done more? It's important, Mark.

You see, I've got a son. He's called Billie. He's just a baby but he doesn't like me. I can tell; always mewling in his cot, turning his face away when I go near him, screaming the place down when I go to pick him up. Luckily, his Dad is good with him. I want to be good with him too. The thing is, I can tell the baby doesn't trust me. I don't blame him.

CHAPTER TWO

I loved you, Mark, I really did, obviously just not enough. If I had done you would still be here. I don't suppose Mum and Dad were too thrilled when the police took them away on suspicion of your murder. Dad was soon in the clear; he had been at work all day and luckily for Mum, even the Man with No Hair had been unable to prove she had been lying when she said she had only left us for a minute.

Mum and Dad weren't gone long, just long enough for me to have to live somewhere else for a while. It was a relief to get out of our house to be honest. After what happened the place creeped me out. I didn't like the people I stayed with. They made me call them Auntie Barbra and Uncle Ray, even though I wasn't related to them. Mum did the same with Porky Rawlings. You were too young to remember but we bumped into him one day when we were out shopping and Mum stood in the middle of the street chatting and laughing with him. When I asked Mum who he was, she went all red and said he was our Uncle Porky. I knew he wasn't; Dad was an only child and Mum didn't have any brothers, just a sister who she didn't like. The name suited him though, with his piggy eyes.

Barbra and Ray never spoke about you. Ever. I wish they had. It would have made a change from hearing her going on about her chilblains. They looked after me well but neither of them showed me any affection, although Barbra did once gave me a quick hug and went a bit watery-eyed on the day of your funeral. I wanted to go but she said I wasn't allowed. She was right, children didn't go to things like that in those days.

I remember the morning the Crow Lady came to collect me. I couldn't wait to leave and was ready and waiting with my bag packed in the hall that Barbra had air-freshened for the occasion. She just stood there, arms folded. I could tell she was pleased I was going. When she wasn't looking, Ray appeared from the living room and pressed two toffees into my palm. I ate them in the car on the way home. They made me feel a bit sick, to be honest.

It was odd being back in the house without you. Someone had taken away all your things: toys, clothes, even your blue flannel had gone from its place on the side of the bath. Mum and Dad carried on as if nothing had happened. She kept her pills well hidden. I looked everywhere, in the cupboard, in her dressing table drawer, I even tried to open the little wooden box underneath her bed but it was locked. I never found the tablets but I knew she was still taking them because I could hear Dad going crazy, threatening to flush them down the toilet. I don't know why he was angry; I was glad she took them. They changed her from Unhappy Mummy to Happy Mummy. Don't get me wrong. The pills didn't always work. Far from it.

Life without you was nothing like I imagined. Mum and Dad hardly ever spoke unless it was to argue about you.

One evening, I heard Mum come home late yet again. I got out of bed and ran to the top of the stairs where I hid behind the banisters. Mum's hair was all mussed up and her lipstick badly smudged. Dad let her have it.

'None of this would've ever happened if it wasn't for you and your bloody tablets.'

'I never touched so much as an aspirin before I met you. He was my son too, you heartless bastard.'

'Son? You'd have to be a mother to have a son. Mother? Scrubber, more like.'

'I did my best.'

'You call leaving a four year old with that bloody idiot, your best?' I knew he meant me.

'You killed him, not me. Remember that,' Dad yelled.

'So, what d'you want me to do? Kill myself?' Mum cried as I heard the familiar sound of the knife drawer being yanked open. You remember, Mark, the one by the sink that made the funny dragging noise.

'Go on then, do us all a favour,' he goaded. 'Here, I'll give you a hand.'

There was a terrible bang and for a minute, I thought Dad had killed her. I ran downstairs. When I reached the third step from the bottom, the one where you used to sit, I waited and watched. Mum was crumpled on the floor, her hair covering one side of her face with Dad standing over her, the veins in his neck sticking out like sticks of rhubarb. I must've made a noise because he suddenly turned to look at me.

'Get back upstairs!'

Before I could move, Mum pushed past me and locked herself in the bathroom, leaving a trail of bloody footprints behind her. The floor had become a frozen lake, covered with broken ice. It made no sense until I saw the hall mirror was no longer on the wall but smashed on the ground.

The next morning Mum got up after Dad had gone to work at the factory and she sat slumped over the table, a cup of tea at her elbow and a cigarette burning in the saucer. Occasionally, she'd pick it up and drag on it as if her life depended on it. Squinting through the smoke, she oozed misery. Without her lipstick and mascara, she didn't look like Mum, just some woman in a nylon dressing gown. I wanted to go to her, hug her and kiss away the lines on her forehead. I hated them; they made her look like an old lady but something about her made me keep my distance.

Then I noticed her feet bound in crepe bandages, the undersides discoloured with bloodstains the size of half crowns. I looked at her face. If she was in pain, she didn't show it.

'Would you like a biscuit, Mummy?' I asked running over and opening the tin.

She looked straight through me. I had become more of a ghost to her than you were. She kept your memory alive with a photograph of you, on her bedside table. Watching from the doorway, I saw how she would hold it carefully by the edge of the frame before kissing your face, forever frozen in a smile behind the glass. Even before you died, I don't ever remember her kissing me.

Dad never spoke about you. In fact, he never mentioned you again.

My dream of stepping into your little leather shoes never happened. I had hoped with just me left to love there would be more to go round but there was less. A lot less.

Mum would even wake up crying. Dad would just get ready and go to work. He never took any time off, not even when you died. Very odd, don't you think? I didn't like leaving Mum when I went to school because I worried about what she might do. For the first couple of weeks, I pretended to have a tummy ache so I could stay at home and keep an eye on her. When Dad found out all hell broke loose. After that, he took me to school himself, dragging me by my arm. I was crying really hard, y'know when you can't stop, your nose is all snotty and it runs into your mouth and you end up swallowing it. Eugh! Dad made it worse, by cuffing me across the head just as we reached the school gates. I think he'd had enough of me by then. My teacher saw him do it but she didn't say anything. I think she was frightened of him too.

Far from our grief bringing the three of us closer together, your death tore us apart. The pain I felt was so bad, I thought it was going to kill me. Obviously, that never happened but it did make me wet the bed. Just like you used to, d'you remember? We slept in that little bed together and when Mum discovered the cold, wet sheets the following morning, I always got the blame. She'd run a freezing bath, then dump me in it, fully clothed. It was supposed to 'teach me a lesson'. It taught me she hated me.

The only person who liked me was some woman who came to the house a few times. Like everyone else, she was more interested in hearing about you than me. She started by asking what games we used to play and what sort of things we spoke about but what she really wanted to know was what had happened the day you died. It took her three visits to get to the point but when she did, she went on and on, question after question. She scribbled down every word I said, filling her notebook with pages of tiny, weird squiggles. I told her everything. Well, almost everything.

Then I said how, after you died, Mum missed you so much she kept threatening to put her head 'in the gas oven'. Even I knew she wouldn't do it; she couldn't, the cooker was electric. I told her Dad never spoke about you. She asked me how that made me feel, not being able to talk about you to anyone. I shrugged and said it was fine because I spoke to you all the time. At first, she didn't get it but then I explained I talked to you, silently, in my head. She smiled at me, put the top back on her pen and the pad in her bag. I was relieved, glad to have got through the session without giving too much away. Just before she got to leave, she reached out and held my hands. Her nails were short and plain, not like Mum's red-polished talons.

'Susan, you know you can tell me anything and I promise I won't be angry with you. I'd just like to ask you one more question but I need you to tell me the truth. Okay?'

I nodded. She was so kind, I'd have agreed to anything she asked.

'Good girl. So, did you love Mark? Did you love your brother?'

I understood the question but not why she asked it. Surely the answer was obvious? All the same I couldn't help thinking, even when you weren't there, it was still all about you. I told her I loved you.

'Cross your heart and hope to die?'

'Yes,' I told her crossing my fingers behind my back, just in case.

Dad must have been listening outside the living room door because when she opened it to leave, he leapt back and looked all flustered. The next few times she turned up, he refused to answer the door and eventually she stopped coming. Shame, I needed a friend. The kids in my class didn't like me and called me names, horrible things, some I didn't even know the meaning of but I could tell by the way they said them they weren't nice. One boy even went so far as to say you weren't dead, just pretending. Some people are just nasty. Luckily, Mark, you weren't around long enough to find out. Dad's temper got worse. One minute, he would be eating his dinner, the next it would be half way up the wall. Mum swapped food for fags, day after day, sitting in bed, filling saucer after saucer with pyramids of cigarette butts. I worried she'd set fire to herself and used to wait for her to fall asleep before creeping in to her room and emptying the overflowing ash down the sink.

One morning, I heard her get up early, straight after Dad had left for work. I hid behind the half-opened bedroom door and watched her. On went her satin conical brassiere, the one that made her look as if she had stepped out of the pages of one of your sci-fi comics, followed by the pink rubber corset and suspenders. She rolled on her stockings, before stepping into her red dress. I waited for her to put on her knickers but she just sat at her dressing table and stared at her reflection in the mirror. Just as she was about to draw on the second eyebrow, she spun round, pencil in hand. I shrunk back but too late. She walked towards me, smiling, her hand outstretched.

'Come on, let's have breakfast.'

It was a lovely thought but even you must remember her idea of breakfast was three cigarettes and a pot of tea.

'Susan,' she said taking my hand.

Coming from her, my name sounded like an angel's. I was so shocked to hear her say it my feet took a while to move. When they did, they followed her excitedly into the kitchen where she sat me on the wooden stool, the same one you had climbed on to get Mum's tablets. I knew because I had marked it with my red crayon, putting a little cross on one side. At last, she was behaving like a real Mum, fussing around, pouring me a glass of milk and arranging custard creams on a plate.

'Don't tell Daddy,' she said with a wink, just like the time she told you not to eat her 'sweets'. 'Dip a biscuit in your milk, go on.'

She picked one up, dunked it, shook off the drops of milk then held it out to me. I hesitated, never quite sure of her. She gave me that look, the one she used to give you, all smiley and happy. How could I refuse? I leant forward and took a bite.

'Nice? Open wide,' she said popping the rest into my mouth. 'Now, you've been such a good girl, I've got a surprise for you.'

I couldn't believe it. The day I had been waiting for all my life had arrived. At last, here we were, just the two of us having fun. She was my Mummy, no-one else's.

'Come on,' she said, lifting me off the stool and setting me down on the floor. 'Race you upstairs!'

I set off after her, feeling happier than I had in a long while. When we got to the landing she ushered me into her bedroom. I stood in the doorway not wanting to go in but she gave me a shove, nothing forceful but enough to make me move. The curtains were still drawn making the room dark and unfriendly. The air smelt of stale cigarette smoke but none of that mattered as I followed her over to the cupboard, you remember, the one where she kept the cardboard tubes containing her rubber corsets. She opened the door. It looked smaller than when we used to play in it. I remember us racing into her room as soon as she went out to dress-up in her clothes. You always went for the fox stole. I never liked it with its black beady eyes. I preferred her dresses, all frills and flowers. They mimicked her shape perfectly. She made sure of that. Every time she bought something new to wear, she would attack it with pins and scissors, snipping out all the excess fabric until it hugged her curves. I longed to try on those dresses but never dared. Knowing my luck I'd have put my foot through a hem or broken a zip. Instead, I settled for emptying out her shoeboxes full of stilettos, sling backs and wedges, all pointy-toed and shiny patent leather. Swopping your sandals for a pair of her high heels, you staggered about, swinging your hips from side to side just like you'd seen Mum do.

'I've taken everything out to give us room to play,' she explained when she saw my quizzical expression at the empty cupboard. 'This can be our secret hiding place, Susan.'

She'd used my name again and she wanted to play with me; what more could I want? I was so happy, for the first time in ages, my tummy stopped hurting. I didn't even need to click my tongue against the roof of my mouth any more.

'What shall we play? I know, hide and seek,' she said, ushering me inside.

'But now you know where I am,' I protested, confused.

'I do but Daddy doesn't,' she said with a wink. 'He'll have to find us both when he comes home.'

When she smiled at me it was the best feeling in the world, like eating warm toast.

'Okay, Susan?' she asked as I nodded enthusiastically.

She was looking at me all funny. I thought perhaps she wanted me to move so she could get in too. I pressed myself against the back of the wardrobe to make room for her and was so excited I let out a little giggle. She put her finger to her lips. Her nails were bright red to match her dress.

'Ssch! Be quiet.'

She widened her eyes, big and black like a cat's. I didn't want to upset her, not with her being so nice.

'I'm going to hide in the garden. Who will Daddy find first when he comes home, d'you think?' she whispered, giving me two biscuits from her dress pocket.

I looked down at the custard creams, wondering how on earth I could eat them quietly.

'Mummy.' Somehow the word escaped. I had spoken it many times in my head but never out loud. It was your name for her. But as you weren't there, I thought it was okay for me to say it. I pursed my lips together, to make the 'M' sound again but her kiss silenced me, her lips briefly brushing my cheek. They were soft and warm, just as I imagined. She stepped back and smiled at me before slamming the door shut.

CHAPTER THREE

I could still smell Mum's perfume. It was like she was in there with me. The sweet sickly scent had clogged in the back of my throat, making it hard to breathe. I wanted to call her name but remembered what she had said about not making a noise. I wasn't sure how Dad would know to come and find us both but I hoped he'd guess we were playing when Mum and I were nowhere to be seen. Just as I was trying to work out how much longer he'd be, I heard Mum's click-clack footsteps going downstairs followed by the sound of the front door opening and closing. I guessed she was off to her hiding place and felt excited and happy to be part of her game.

I wondered whereabouts in the garden she would go. There weren't many good places to hide, no sheds or big trees, just patches of grass all sunburnt and brown. There was that bush, you remember the one with the yellow leaves just under the kitchen window, but it wasn't nearly big enough and Dad would easily spot her red dress through the branches.

I peeped through the crack in the door and could just make out her bed covered with the green candlewick bedspread, the one you were sick on that time. It wasn't your fault. You were just a baby, six months, maybe. Mum was asleep and you were crying your head off. The last thing I needed was for her to wake up and start shouting at me. So I gave you some milk. Before I knew what was happening, you'd drunk the whole bottle and thrown up all over the bed. I tried to clean it off with my flannel before Mum saw it but I can't have done a very good job because it always smelt a bit cheesy after that. I looked at the dressing table. There was something different about it. I couldn't work out what at first, then realised the creams and potions Mum used to make herself look less like a mum and more like a film star, had disappeared. For once, I could see the surface with its scratches and overlapping ring marks. I should have known something was wrong but I just thought she'd had one of her clear-outs and thrown the lot away. She was always doing that. Once, I'd gone to bed and left my doll in the living room. Mum gave it away. Can you believe it? She didn't even tell me. That afternoon, I spotted the girl over the road playing with it. Funny how Mum could always afford the latest make-up yet when I asked for something like a new pencil case or hair ribbons, she always told me we had no money.

'Want, want, want, don't keep on. You should be grateful you don't live in Africa. The kids are starving out there. You're not underfed. Anyone can see that.'

Nothing she could say back then could stop me loving her. I watched happily as she sat in front of her huge dressing table mirror, her hair in pink plastic rollers, quilted nylon dressing-gown buttoned up to her neck, as she leant forward to transform her face in a blur of brushes, powder and paint. I didn't know it then but looking back, it was all for Porky Rawlings' benefit. She was playing Dad for a mug even then.

Anyway, you don't want to know about all that. What I'm telling you is far more important. It matters, Mark. Please listen.

Waiting for Dad to come and find me, I was bored, really bored. You know, like we used to be every Sunday when everything was closed and there was nothing to do. It's all so different now. You can't imagine. Sunday is no longer a day of rest, just the opposite. All the shops are open; you can do whatever you want. But back then, when we were little, time dragged didn't it? We never went anywhere as a family. Dad would get all dressed up and go out and Mum slept all day.

I was still clutching the biscuits Mum had given me. I halved one, carefully sliding off the top so I could make it last longer by licking the icing off first. It was getting hot in there and I needed the toilet, badly. I tried to take my mind off it by trying to picture Mum hiding in the garden. It was odd but I couldn't imagine her without you by her side. Funny how I thought more about you after you died than when you were alive. You never left me Mark, not for a minute. Just need you to know. Stuff like that's important. I know that now.

Sorry, where was I? Oh, yes, I missed you and wanted to talk to you. I wanted to ask you what it was like in heaven. Did you get to meet other dead people? And if you did, were they the same as you remembered or did they look different? Not that you'd have recognised your grandparents, we never met them or even saw their photo. I wondered if you'd seen Dennis-from-across-the-road and whether he still had asthma. I couldn't imagine all that coughing and wheezing in heaven.

'Mark, are you there?' I whispered.

Straightaway, your laughter seemed to echo around me. I wasn't frightened. Well, I was a bit but once I started to imagine what you might say to me, I was fine. You told me Dennis was better and could run about with the other kids. It was good to know he was happy, at last. Then, before I got chance to ask

23

any more questions, you told me about a new friend you'd made, Gillian. You couldn't stop talking about her, telling me how pretty she was with her blue eyes and long brown hair. Straightaway, I knew who she was because I remembered seeing her picture in Dad's paper. She had been murdered on her way home from school, just a few miles from where we lived. It was funny to think of you, without me. You made heaven sound like a playground that never closed. I was just happy you were happy. Honest.

I really needed to pee but I didn't want to leave the wardrobe in case Dad came home and spotted me. I put my hand between my legs and squeezed but it just made it worse. I wished Dad would hurry up and come home. Sometimes he was in when I got back from school, other days I didn't see him until the next morning. There was no way I could hold on. Suddenly, my legs were wet. It felt nice at first, all warm. But then the wee ran into my shoes and made my feet cold. Quickly, I stuffed the last biscuit into my mouth then took off my shoes, socks and knickers. I balled my pants into my socks and used the bundle as a makeshift sponge in an attempt to clean up the puddle. I thought about Mum again, all alone in the garden, freezing in her sleeveless dress. I hoped she had remembered to put her coat on before she went out. Surely, she was bound to be wearing her jacket, the one with the fur collar? I pictured her with it zipped up to her chin, waiting for Dad.

I missed you. Talking to you in my head was okay but I wanted you with me in that cupboard. You always had the best ideas. You'd have turned it into a castle to escape from or a bank to rob, even a magician's box to do tricks in. Life was dull without you and I only had myself to blame. I should've stopped you taking those tablets when I had the chance.

24

'I wish I was in heaven with you, Mark. Can I come up to play, just for a bit? I won't stay long, promise.'

To my surprise, you answered straightaway.

'No, silly, you're not allowed.'

'Why not?'

I waited and waited but you didn't reply.

The sides of the cupboard were moving in on me, I was sure of it. I put my hands out and tried to push them back but they wouldn't budge. It was getting hard to breathe and I was sure I could smell smoke. Perhaps, one of Mum's cigarette butts had tumbled off the stack in the ash-tray and was burning its way through the carpet. I knew she'd set fire to the place one day. I told myself not to worry, if the house did go up in flames, Mum would rescue me. Obviously, if you'd still been here, she would have saved you first and I would have had to take my chances but not anymore. Now, there was only me to look after.

I was gasping for air and leant against the door, pushing with all my might. It wouldn't budge. It must've got stuck when Mum shut it. I started yelling and banging so hard on the wood, my knuckles stung. No wonder, I'd pulled the skin off. Suppose something bad happened while I was stuck in there, like a burglar broke in? Then what? I bashed on the door again. What was the point? No one could hear me. Mum was outside and the next-door neighbour was at work. You must remember him, you liked him because he was a bus-driver and every time he saw you he said you could have a go in his cab. You got all excited but he never kept his promise. Lucky you. Anyway, sometimes he worked late shifts and slept during the day. Mum used to tell us to be quiet so as not to wake him. But, I knew he wasn't at home because I'd overheard him telling Mum the previous morning that we could make as much noise as we liked because he would be at work all day. It had started to spit with rain and she'd run into the garden to get the washing in. He didn't spot me but I could see him, leaning over the fence, watching her as she unpegged the clothes from the line. I didn't understand why he would want to stand out there, staring at her, getting wet. Looking back it was a shame Dad hadn't seen. He'd have killed him.

Back in the wardrobe, my tummy began to ache. I'd had the pain before when Mum had made me eat some rice pudding that had been hanging about for days. I tried to hold on, I really did but it was no use. I had to stand on tip-toes to avoid the mess I'd made. The stench was so terrible I lifted up my top to cover my nose and mouth. I don't know how long it was before I heard Dad's key in the front door but I remember it made me cry. I thought he'd go mad when he saw what I'd done. I could hear him moving around downstairs, going from room to room, calling out for Mum. When she didn't answer he headed upstairs.

'S-S-Susan, where are you?' I didn't like the way he said my name. He couldn't pronounce his 's's properly and made a hissing sound, like a snake.

'I'm here, in the cupboard,' I shouted, relieved.

His footsteps quickened. Then, I heard him outside and the key turning. Mum had locked me in. What had she done that for? I wasn't going to cheat or find another hiding place. Dad jumped back as the mess I'd made seeped out all over his shoes. For a moment, he didn't react, just stared at me. When, he lifted his hand, I thought he was going to hit me and jerked away. He pulled the neck of his T-shirt up over his mouth and nose before scooping me up. He held me tight, not caring I was making his new cardigan, the cream one with the brown leather buttons, all wet. Embarrassed, I wriggled and struggled, desperate to get down. Without a word, he carried me into the bathroom and started to undress me. Only Mum had ever seen me naked before. That was fine; we were both girls. I pulled my skirt around me so he couldn't reach the buttons. I think he understood because he immediately let go and turned away. I took off my jumper so quickly I pulled my vest off with it. Then I undid my skirt and let it fall to the floor. For a moment, I was shocked to see I wasn't wearing any knickers then remembered I'd left them in the wardrobe where I'd used them as a cloth. I stepped into the bath, careful to keep my back to Dad. I started to shake, really shiver, but I wasn't cold. Dad attached the plastic shower hose to the taps and checked the temperature of the water on his hand before hosing me down. Then he handed me the soap to wash myself. When you were here, Mum bathed and dressed you first. I had to use your water. It was always cold and grey by the time I got in.

Dad wrapped me in a towel before going to the airing cupboard for a clean nightie. It felt lovely and warm when I put it on.

'Okay?' he asked. That was it. He didn't want to know what had happened or where Mum was or even how long I'd been locked in the wardrobe. 'S-S-Susan, you alright?'

I wasn't but I nodded all the same. It was easiest. That was the thing with Mum and Dad, neither of them wanted to know what I felt.

That day, Dad had been in no hurry to find Mum. In fact, I don't think he even bothered looking. It was like he didn't care where she was or even whether she was coming back. I watched him that evening, pottering about making the pair of us a pot of tea, something I'd never seen him do before. To my surprise, he knew exactly what to do. He boiled the kettle, warmed the pot, put in two spoonfuls of tea plus an extra one. Then he set out two cups and saucers, both chipped but that didn't matter. It was just good he was actually doing something nice for me. Using a strainer to catch the leaves, he poured the tea, adding a dash of milk to both before stirring in three heaped spoonfuls of sugar and handing me the drink.

'Mind, it's hot,' he warned.

It tasted really sweet, like it had been made with golden syrup. He offered me the biscuit barrel. It was full of custard creams, just like the ones Mum had given me. I threw up in the tin. For once, he wasn't cross, just took the container outside and threw it in the bin. Then, he locked both the back and front doors, telling me not to let anyone in. I knew he meant Mum.

She must have discovered a good hiding place because we never did find her.

CHAPTER FOUR

After that, it was just Dad and me. Or should it be 'me and Dad'? Or 'Dad and I'? I don't know. Y'see, Mark, after you'd gone, I never paid much attention at school. I hated the place and was hardly ever there. Dad didn't know, well not for ages. I used to get ready and leave with him when he went to work. I'd wait until he was out of sight, then chuck my bag over a hedge and take off for the day. I had no money so I couldn't do much. Just spent the time lurking in shop doorways or hiding in the park worried in case someone who knew Dad spotted me. Still it beat sitting in class, bored to death. Sorry, I didn't mean to say that word, death. I don't want to upset you any more than I already have. If it was raining, I'd go to school but it was embarrassing because I was always behind the rest of the class, and the other kids bullied me. Paul Brown was the worst. He made up chants, nasty, horrible stuff. He must've heard other people gossiping because he would have been too young to understand what he was saying.

'Your brother's dead and your Mum's in bed...with the barman.' The last bit didn't rhyme but that didn't bother Paul Brown who was twice the size of most of the other boys in our class and the self-appointed leader of the pack. Even Clarkie, the Headmaster, was scared of him, never daring to tell him off.

One day, he started on me again. 'Your brother's dead and your Mum's in bed with the barman, the butcher, the baker and the candlestick-maker.' The anger never had a chance to build. It shot straight up through me, like a flame. I stood up, and threw my chair across the room. I was aiming for Paul Brown's fat head but he ducked and just stood there laughing at me as the chair clattered to the floor. The teacher knew he was to blame. She'd heard him taunting me but instead of punishing him, she sent me to the headmaster's office.

Tears of fury and indignation welled up but I was determined not to let Clarkie see me cry. I stood there, in his room that smelt of sweat and furniture polish, saying nothing. There was no point trying to explain why I'd done it. I could see by his reflection in the glass doors of the bookcase he wasn't interested. He wasn't even looking at me. I turned to look at him. His hair looked like a piece of steamed haddock, the sort that's dyed orange. Guess that's what years of smoking does for you. Not that I ever saw him with a cigarette but his nicotine-stained fingers were a dead giveaway. Sorry, I've done it again, haven't I? I've used the 'D' word. He put me on detention every night for a week. No way was I sticking around for that. I legged it and didn't go back for ages. That's why I ended up missing loads more lessons including the one about whether it's 'me and Dad' or 'Dad and me'. Then again, nothing was ever about Dad and me. There was me. And there was Dad. And that was that.

After he'd rescued me from the cupboard I had hoped things would be better between us. That night, we had a good evening, all things considered. He made me dinner. Well, he burnt a frozen pie. Guess his mind was on other things. The pastry was all black and smoking when he eventually pulled it out of the oven, his hand wrapped in the tea-towel, the blue one, the one you had used to unscrew the lid from the pill bottle. Swearing, he had thrown the charred mess into the sink, running the cold tap and making a great whoosh of steam appear. He pushed the soggy meat and pastry down the plughole with the point of a knife. It took him forever, poking and prodding. When he was satisfied every last trace had disappeared he gave me a bowl of cornflakes with sugar but no milk. What little was left in the bottle had separated into two layers. That went down the sink too. For pudding, we had peaches; not just a spoonful like Mum used to give me but the whole tin between us. They were lovely, sweet and syrupy. Dad even let me sit up late with him. We didn't do anything special but it didn't matter. For once, it was just Dad and me.

All I can think is that with you and Mum gone, Dad felt like he was stuck with me because after that night he was different, really different. Of the three of us, you, me and Mum, I was the last person he would have chosen to be left with. You would have been his first choice, no doubt about that. I'm sure he would've have even tolerated Mum for a bit longer too. Believe it or not, I think he loved her. I know they were always rowing but I still remember the way he used to look at her. He used to follow her about like a puppy. It got on her nerves; I could see that. The trouble was, I think he liked her more than she liked him. He must've known she was up to no good. Even I knew something was wrong and I was only little. She used to get all dolled up, then clear off, all night sometimes. You won't remember but I used to lie awake, long after you'd gone to sleep, just waiting for the sound of her key in the door. Y'see, I couldn't rest until I knew she was home safe. When I eventually heard her staggering upstairs, I'd get out of bed, tiptoe to the door and peer through the crack, always careful never to let her see me. One time, I saw her limp upstairs wearing only one shoe. Her stockings were in holes and she was cussing underneath her breath. Back then, I'd never heard the words before and had no idea what they meant.

Dad must have loved her very much to put up with it. Perhaps 'love' is too strong a word. I don't know. I wasn't in his head. Or hers. Love is an odd thing. Y'see Mark, often the people you love, don't love you back. It's not fair; it's just the way it is. And the people you should hold in your heart forever somehow slip away. I've never been able to work that one out. I know I cramped Dad's style.

The next-door-neighbour knocked one evening, a few weeks after Mum disappeared, and asked Dad if he fancied going to the pub. He thought about it, even got so far as to grab his coat, but then he shook his head and closed the door. He should've gone, that way at least one of us would have had a good time. Instead he just sat in his chair, giving off this horrible vibe. That's another weird thing, Mark, some people can tell you everything they want you to know by saying absolutely nothing. Neither of us spoke much. It was hard to think of things to talk about when all we had in common was you and Mum, one dead and one missing, hardly the stuff to fill our house with laughter.

What did fill the space was an elephant. We had an elephant in the room. Not a real one, obviously. It's just an expression, something people say when there's a big problem that everyone knows about but nobody mentions. Who do you think the elephant could be? Go on, have a guess. Don't know? It was you, Mark. You were the elephant in the room.

If I looked like I might say something, anything, Dad would shut down the conversation, just in case I mentioned you. His favourite method was to hide behind his Daily Mirror, gripping the pages between his big, calloused hands, his fingers twitching like he was playing the accordion. I couldn't bear it. My insides would knot with frustration. I wanted to tell him what had happened that day but he was having none of it, his face hidden behind the headlines, lost in someone else's sob story.

As time went on, he took to working longer hours. If our empty fridge was anything to go by, we needed the money. We lived on frozen chips. I know that must sound great to you but trust me, after a while you get sick of them. Dad lost weight, his clothes hung off him and he didn't look like Dad anymore, with his hollow cheeks and sunken eyes. He unnerved me and I was glad he was hardly ever at home. It was a relief. You never knew what was going on inside his head. A bit like Mum, I suppose. I don't know why I'm telling you all this. You probably can't even hear me, can you? Well, say something. I know you're there, hanging on my every word because you want to find out what happened that day as much as I need to tell you. Oh Mark, I'm sorry. I'm just trying to be honest with you. After all this time, that's the least I owe you. Please listen, I promise not to shout at you again.

With you gone, I hated being in the house and took to visiting the library. At first, it wasn't so much about reading but avoiding Dad. It was warm in there and I could stay for hours. I liked the silence. And there was no danger of Paul Brown popping in to torment me. The librarian gave me a special membership card that I showed every time I borrowed a book. It made me feel important. I liked the Reading Room best. It was brilliant, all the newspapers, including the big posh ones, were there to read, for free. At first, I just stuck to The Daily Mirror because it had lots of pictures. It took me a while but I soon worked out how to piece together the stories, especially those that ran for a few days. It was easy to work out who the bad guy was. His picture was made up of strips of other people's faces: one man's hair, another's eyes, someone else's nose and a different man's mouth. It was called a photo-fit. If I squinted I could imagine what the suspect might look like. The victim was usually a child or a young woman. Obviously, because I didn't know what all the words meant I missed out on chunks of the story. It was frustrating so I watched what other people did. If they were unsure of a word they looked it up in the dictionary, a book full of words and their meanings. I did the same and each week I discovered something new. It was hard at first but soon I could read, not brilliantly but enough to get by.

As the weeks went by, I started to really enjoy it and soon became familiar with the famous faces that appeared week after week on the front pages. There was always a funny-looking man with a pipe. Apparently, he was the Prime Minister, a very important person called Harold Wilson. He ran the country, which surprised me because I'd always thought the Queen was in charge. He used to go on about the 'pound in your pocket'. Pound? I was lucky if I had a penny in mine. To my young mind, Harold Wilson was very boring. Murders were more my thing. The stories often ran for weeks, covering the first report of the missing person, the discovery of the body, the arrest of the killer and eventually their trial. I read every word and used to get this weird feeling inside when I discovered exactly how they had killed their victims, sort of half scared, half excited.

Don't get me wrong, I liked other stuff too, especially cartoons. My favourite was 'The Perishers', a family of children who roamed the streets with a baby in a pram and survived on their wits without an adult in sight.

The librarian used to see me most days and suggested a few books I might like. At first I didn't enjoy them because there were no pictures but after a while I imagined my own. It was magic, sitting there conjuring up wonderful scenes, visiting places I'd never heard of, meeting people from the past, even making new friends. Before I knew it, a weird thing happened. I started writing, nothing much at first, just a few lines. I'd look through the papers to give me ideas for stories and used to sit in the Reading Room, writing for hours. I decided to go back to school. I had something I wanted to show the English teacher. She couldn't believe it when I proudly handed her my first ever essay, entitled 'What puts a smile on my face'. It was a title I remembered her giving us at the beginning of term. I had no idea how to approach it back then but armed with my new-found knowledge, the story all but wrote itself. Sitting at the table in the library, I had known exactly what I was going to write, every word balanced in my head waiting to tumble onto the paper. Considering I was putting it all down so quickly my handwriting wasn't too bad; you could read it, just about. It was well worth the effort. The teacher gave me ten out of ten and was so pleased she did a big red tick from the bottom of the page to the top. Paul Brown said I must have copied the story from someone else but my teacher knew better. No one else could have written it because it was all about you.

From that day, I loved school. Well I wasn't much good at maths but I loved English. Writing was a great way of getting rid of all the words and feelings that upset me. Dumping down my thoughts was my way of dealing with them and moving on. I could write whatever I wanted, lie if it made me feel better. Only it's not called lying when you write, it's called using your imagination. I did a lot of that. Made up all sorts. I was very good at it. Sometimes, I'd reread the story and even I couldn't tell which bits were true and which parts were imaginary. Y'see, Mark, the trouble with writing is it doesn't help you to forget, it forces you to remember every last detail. But writing does allow you to forgive yourself absolutely anything.

At first, writing was hard work, going over and over stuff, deciding what to put in and what to leave out but before long, my essays were the best in the class. They were so good the teacher read them out in the lesson. All the other kids couldn't believe I had turned into a brainbox overnight. Even Paul Brown developed a grudging respect for me and found someone else to bully. Like I said, I loved school. I would've slept there if I could. Home was too big and cold without you. Dad was in his own world, a crazy place that I couldn't and didn't want to enter. I remember showing him my English book once. Obviously, I didn't let him read any of my essays but he saw all the ticks, stars and full marks. I thought he'd be pleased, proud even but all he said was, 'Is that it?' I never showed him anything after that.

It wasn't his fault, I suppose. Apart from the Daily Mirror, I never saw him read. There were no books in the house. When Mum left, Dad threw out all her magazines. *Titbits* and *Weekend* were her favourites. Cup of tea in one hand, fag in the other, she devoured every word. She couldn't get enough of stories like, 'My night with a Vampire' and 'Street of a Thousand Sins'. There was never any chance of me sitting on her knee and learning my ABC.

Dad was never bothered about her leaving. Even the day she disappeared, I don't think he rang the police. If he did, they never came round the house like they did the night you died. It was as if he knew she was never coming home. At first, I thought he'd killed her and buried her under that bush in the garden. I even went so far as to picture the black soil falling off his spade, covering her red dress as she lay lifeless in the freshly dug grave.

I was all set to write a story about it when a letter arrived addressed to Dad.

Immediately, I recognised Mum's handwriting. I held it up to the light and could just make out row upon row of tightknit scribble. Mum wasn't one to put pen to paper very often, so it must've taken her ages to put a letter together. Even after everything that had happened, I was relieved she was still alive and left the envelope on the table for Dad to see when he got up. He never bothered to open it, just took one look and binned it. If you'd asked me then whether I loved her after everything she'd done, I don't know what I'd have said. Her locking me in a cupboard and then doing a runner wasn't great but that's the thing about life Mark, just when you think it can't get any worse, it does.

You may not believe me and I wouldn't blame you if you didn't, but losing you was and still is the most awful thing that has happened to me. Not even what I'm about to tell you was that bad.

CHAPTER FIVE

I was eight years old and should have known better. That's what Dad said when he found out.

I have never told anyone what happened apart from him and that nosey old police-woman with the leaky pen, who wrote down every embarrassing word I said. I hated the way I was left alone with someone I'd never met, forced to tell her things I didn't understand.

Now, I'm about to tell you, not because I want to but because I need you to know how your death changed my life. Y'see if you'd been with me, none of this would have happened. Not that I'm blaming you; I'm just saying.

It was the summer of '67. Stories that begin like that are usually about lazy, sunny days. Good times. Times you hope will never end but what I'm about to tell you is nothing like that. So, I'll start again.

It was a Monday, the first day of the long school holidays and it was already shaping up to be another sweltering morning. Our house was bang in the middle of a long row of red brick terraced houses and consequently absorbed the heat like a giant clay oven. It was ten past ten. I remember the exact time because when I woke up, I looked at the clock and thought it said ten to two. I panicked, rushed out of bed and ran downstairs in my nightdress, thinking I had missed most of the day. If only I had.

I was looking forward to enjoying toast, with butter and jam, in bed. I wasn't allowed food in my room. Dad always insisted I ate at the kitchen table but he would never know; he was at work. I turned on the cold tap and drank from it, something else he would never let me do. Wiping my mouth with the back of my hand, I looked through the kitchen window to see next-door's cat in our back garden. She was squatting, doing her business on the circle of cracked, dried mud that used to be a flowerbed before Dad gave up tending it. When she had finished, she turned round, pawing repeatedly at the hard soil, doing her best to try and cover her mess. I liked her and often let her in when Dad was out. He hated cats; thought they were dirty and would always chase them off. I tapped on the glass, she looked up and blinked at me, her pupils thin black slits in the morning sun. I opened the door and she shot inside, making a beeline for me, stepping out a figure of eight, around my legs, rubbing her soft fur against my calves. She started to meow. I knew that cry. She wanted feeding. As usual, the fridge was empty but I had heard the milkman earlier, the chink of bottles like a dawn chorus, only tardier. Our milkman was not an early bird. With the cat trotting beside me, I ran down the corridor and opened the front door. The bottle of silver top was just out of my reach. As I stepped outside to get it, the door blew shut behind me. After giving it a shove, just in case the lock hadn't quite caught, I bent down and flipped open the letter-box even though I knew it was pointless. What was I expecting, the cat to come and let me in? Sitting in the hallway, oblivious to my plight, she washed herself, working her paw over her ear. When she caught me spying on her, she walked away, her tail in the

40

air. I felt let down, like there was some way she could have helped me if only she'd tried. I let the flap clatter shut.

What was I going to do, locked out in my nightie? I began to panic and could feel the sweat running in rivulets down my back. Then, I remembered; I hadn't locked the back door after I'd let the cat in. Thank goodness! All I had to do was find a way into my back garden. You remember how the houses were tightly packed and there were no alleyways. The only way was to go through a neighbour's house and over their fence and the only one I knew was Mr Blake, you remember the bus driver, the one I was telling you about before? He might be at work but I'd give it a go and if he wasn't in, I could always ask the people on the other side. I didn't know them but this was an emergency.

Dad had always told me never to speak to strangers. It was just one of those things he said, like 'Don't run across the road', 'Don't play with matches' and 'Don't take sweets from men in cars.' I never got that, where was the harm in a few toffees? Surely if they were kind enough to offer, it was rude to refuse?

Anyway, none of that mattered, Mr Blake wasn't a stranger, he was our neighbour and most importantly, Tom and Kevin's dad. You won't remember them; you were too young. You'd have liked them. Tom was nine years old and Kevin ten. They didn't live next door. They stayed with their Mum during the week but visited their Dad most weekends. They were the only other kids I knew whose parents had separated. We never spoke about it; we didn't need to. Unlike Paul Brown, they didn't bully me or ask stupid questions. We just played together, either in my back garden or theirs but never out the front. None of us were allowed in the street. I liked Tom the best because he shared his gum with me. I used to copy him and lean against the wall, one leg bent up behind me, chewing away thinking I looked cool. Kevin used to show off and blow bubbles, big pink clouds that when he blew too hard, burst like balloons all over his face. I always knew when the pair of them had arrived because I'd hear Kevin kicking his football against the fence.

Anyway, as I was saying, there I was in the street, desperate to get inside before someone saw me. I walked straight up Mr Blake's path, careful not to tread on the dandelions growing through the cracks in the concrete like bursts of sunshine. It seemed mean to trample on them after all their efforts and I watched where I put my feet. Momentarily distracted by a patch of once verdant grass that had browned in the heat, I did the very thing I had been trying to avoid and trod on a dandelion. I bent down and touched it, the sap seeping out and staining the inside of my fingers.

Standing in the porch, the rough coir matting pricking the soles of my bare feet, I was in the full glare of the sun and could feel the heat pricking my back through the thin cotton. Should I disturb Mr Blake? Supposing he was asleep and I woke him up? Dad would be furious if he found out. Just as I was about to retrace my steps, two teenage girls in denim shorts swaggered past, smoking one cigarette between them. I shrank back, hoping they wouldn't spot me. Too late, I had already caught the taller one's eye. She nudged her friend, and they both laughed. That did it. I wasn't going to stand there to be made a fool of. I pushed the doorbell. Then, pressed it again, harder. I waited, shifting my weight impatiently from foot to foot. 'Please be in, please be in,' I thought, willing the girls to go away. Suddenly the door opened and there stood Mr Blake. Far from being annoyed, he looked delighted to see me.

'Hello Susan, what a lovely surprise,' he said, his bright tone reflected in his luminous orange shirt and blue trousers. He was dressed; at least I hadn't woken him. 'Tom and Kevin aren't here. They're with their Mum, caravanning in Kent.' He smiled and went to close the door.

'No, please,' I said panicking. 'I'm sorry to bother you but I went out to get the milk in and locked myself out.'

When he didn't reply, I filled the silence by clicking my tongue against the roof of my mouth. Then, I started talking, too fast, stumbling over my words. 'Dad's at work. He won't be back for ages but it's okay because when I let the cat in I left the back door open. It's not my cat; I just feed it.' I stared at my feet, having run out of things to say. Speaking to adults made me nervous. I didn't do it often. He watched me, the corners of his mouth twitching, like he was trying to suppress a smirk.

'I'm guessing you want to climb over my fence?' He gave me an indulgent smile, the sort grown-ups reserve for children when they want to make them feel, well, childish. 'Come in, Susan. Go straight through,' he said opening the door fully and ushering me inside. He was a big man. His size meant I had to turn sideways to get by. 'That's right. Straight down the corridor and into the kitchen,' he instructed pointing along the long, narrow hall.

I breathed in and edged past him. It was the first time I had ever been inside his house. The kitchen was clean and smelt oddly familiar. Then, I remembered, it was the way you used to smell when you were a baby, all fresh and clean. Perhaps he used the same washing powder as Mum did back then. I could

43

just picture you in your blue spaceman pyjamas and smiled to myself.

'It's hot isn't it?' he suddenly exclaimed. 'Would you like a drink?' Beads of sweat gathered on his forehead. Wiping them away with one hand, he reached for a glass from the draining board with the other. I couldn't help noticing his nails. They were very clean, not like Dad's, black and bitten. 'Orange squash or I might have some lemonade somewhere?'

'Neither thank you,' I replied, eyeing the fence through the window.

You probably don't remember it but it wasn't very high. If I tucked my nightie into my knickers, I could easily climb over it. I would just have to be careful not to get splinters in my feet or hands. He caught my eye and smiled, putting the glass down and running his hand over his head, as smooth and speckled as a hen's egg. He reached inside the cupboard and took out an unopened bottle of squash. I watched as he slowly unscrewed the top and poured a little of the thick orange liquid into the clear tumbler. We didn't have glasses at home, only mismatched cups and saucers and most of those were chipped.

'D'you like it strong?' he persisted, bottle poised.

I had no idea how I liked it. Dad always made me drink water. According to him, bottled drinks were a waste of money, unlike the beer he got through of an evening after he had sent me to bed. I used to lie awake for hours listening to him downstairs. Once, I even thought I heard him cry.

'I must go, Mr Blake,' I said.

'Have this first,' he said hastily topping up the glass with cold water from the tap and holding it out to me. 'Here, Susan, take it.' He was doing his best to sound kind but his voice had developed a hard edge. I moved towards the back door.

'It's locked. You can't be too careful these days, some very funny people about. Wait here, I'll get the key.'

He raced off leaving me wondering why the back door key wasn't kept near the back door. I looked around. There was no evidence of Mark or Kevin. I thought there might at least be some muddy football boots lying around. It's funny but to this day, I don't recall seeing a cooker, a table or even a chair. But I'll never forget the built-in seat underneath the window. Covered in a red shiny fabric, it was so wide it seemed to fill the entire room. I was just wondering if it was where Tom and Kevin slept when Blake reappeared.

Naked.

He was naked but for a small yellow towel knotted at his waist. In that moment he became someone I didn't know. He had become a stranger. I found myself staring and immediately looked away. My feet were sweating, sticking to the linoleum.

'Please, Mr Blake, I'd like to go now.' My voice came out all thin and reedy. I didn't dare say too much because I knew if I did, I'd start to cry. I hated being polite but I didn't want to upset him.

He didn't reply, simply lowered himself onto the padded seat and as he did the towel rode up and parted, revealing the top of his thighs. My heart was thumping loudly but if he heard it, he did not let on. He simply patted the space beside him. I wanted to run but was unable to move. Besides, the room was so small he could be on me in a moment.

'I... want... to... go... home.'

He splayed his hands to show me his empty palms. 'Couldn't find the key. Besides no-one's at home, are they Susan?'

45

'My Daddy...' As I spoke his name, I tried to imbue it with a magical strength that would make Blake recoil in terror.

'Your Daddy is at work. You told me, remember? And we both know he won't be home for hours, don't we? Since your little brother died, terrible business that, and your Mum left you, I've noticed your Daddy is hardly ever at home.'

How dare he mention you? I hated that other people knew your tale, the one that must have been told many times, embellished by careless gossips with nothing better to do. Someone laughed; a horrible tight little snort. It was me.

'Not frightened, are you?' he whispered, leaning back.

I shook my head but inside I was terrified. I bet you're wondering why I didn't scream or cry for help, aren't you? Well, I didn't think anyone would hear me and I didn't dare. It's hard to explain. It's like most things in life; you don't get it until it happens to you. I can only tell you what I did and how I felt. I stood still, silently begging him not to touch me. Tears welled up and almost spilled out, but I squeezed them back in. Then I counted in my head, just like I did that day in the wardrobe. 'One, two, three, by the time I get to ten this will be over,' I told myself.

He was still stretched out on the seat. Whorls of dark brown hair covered his chest and stomach, odd given he had none on his head. I had never seen a bare-chested man. Dad wasn't the sort to wander around the house in just his underwear and I never saw anyone else because we never went to a swimming pool let alone a beach.

Blake's eyes were closed but he wasn't asleep. Far from it. He was lying with his feet flat on the bed, his knees bent, the towel discarded beside him. I had no idea what he was doing to himself or why. I just knew it wasn't right and I had to get out.

I was more frightened than I had ever been. Again, I tried to convince myself just by counting to ten in my head, I could make it all go away. 'One, two...'

'Watch, Susan,' he ordered, opening his eyes to look at me.

I refused and concentrated on the numbers, '...three, four, five, six,...'

'Susan, look!'

'...seven, eight, nine...'

Then, I heard him laugh.

'Ten,' I breathed out loud. It acted like some sort of alarm, causing him to leap up, all flustered and embarrassed. He fumbled for the towel, his fingers worked to secure it around his waist. It was too late for modesty. It was too late for anything.

'Please, let me go.' My voice came out so softly, I wasn't sure whether I had actually spoken the words or just thought them. But he must have heard me because he walked over to the door and turned the handle. It had been open all along. I ran forward. Thankfully, he made no attempt to stop me as I squeezed past, careful not to brush against him but he lent towards me and I felt his knee touch my thigh through my nightie.

'Promise not to tell anyone?' he asked, puffing his horrible vinegary breath in my face. 'Our little secret, eh, Susan.'

I ran into the garden and scrambled like a rabbit chased by a fox over the fence. After stumbling into the house, I bolted the door behind me and switched on the radio, desperate to hear a voice that was not Blake's. Music blared out and I turned the volume up as loud as it would go. Choking on my own tears, I

47

curled up under the table and locked my arms over my eyes, wishing away the things I had seen. By the time Dad came home, I was on the sofa, watching television, like nothing had happened. I never said a word. I was too worried what Blake would do to me if I did.

But I knew, one day I'd have my revenge. Y'see Mark, I owned the most deadly weapon in the world, one I could use anytime I wanted. My pen.

CHAPTER SIX

I kept it a secret all over the summer holidays. I had to. I felt dirty and couldn't face the thought of Dad knowing. Thankfully, he never suspected. As you know, Dad and I could go for days without talking, so me not saying much was nothing new. Besides, there was no point, not really. He couldn't undo what had happened. The images still lurk in the shadows, ready to hijack my mind at any moment. I can be having the best time, without a care in the world, and they'll suddenly appear, as vivid and vile as ever. Anyway, Dad wasn't interested. He wasn't even bothered about how I was doing at school or who my friends were. Not that I had many. Most of the kids avoided me after you died. It was as if they thought death was contagious, like a cold. It was weird but I got used to it. Evenings and weekends were the worst with Dad, hour after boring hour, with him just sat in that chair, you remember, the one next to the gas fire, hidden behind his paper, emitting the occasional cough or disapproving tut.

'What are you doing?' he would ask, unable to conceal his annoyance, when he got up to go to the toilet or perform some other such humdrum activity.

'Reading.'

'Don't lie.' An odd response given he could see the pile of books at my feet. I showed him what I was studying once:

poems by Walter de la Mare and Robert Louis Stevenson. My favourite was the one about flowers; hollyhocks and foxgloves, plants I had never heard of, let alone seen. Each verse was illustrated with pencil sketches. Dad had liked gardening once and I thought he might be interested but he took one look and walked off. I shouldn't have taken it personally; Dad didn't speak to anyone if he could help it.

So, imagine my surprise when one Saturday afternoon, I went into the garden to find him talking to Blake across the very same fence I had clambered over that horrific afternoon. I put my head down and made straight for the shed where I pretended to be busy getting out my bicycle but all the time I was listening to every word. They were chatting about boring stuff like the weather. I couldn't believe the nerve of that bastard. Then, he spoke to me, as calm as you like.

'Hello, Susan.'

Of course, I ignored him. Well, Dad wasn't having any of that and gave me one of his looks. Blake saw and sniggered, a nasty, sarcastic little snort. I glared at him with such force I hoped he might spontaneously combust. No such luck. Dad just told me to stop being so rude. 'Apologise to Mr Blake,' Dad roared, his cheeks all red.

I couldn't believe it. I was expected to say sorry to him? It was wrong, very wrong. My whole body burned with injustice and I could feel myself getting angry. I had nothing to apologise to him for and said as much. If anything, he should be saying sorry to me. Both men turned to stare at me as if wondering what I was going to say next. Even I wasn't entirely sure. Perhaps I should just shut up but with Dad standing next to me, I felt ridiculously confident; Dad was terrifying, Blake wouldn't dare do anything. And this time I was on my side of the fence, I could run indoors away from him anytime I wanted. If I spoke up, I could be free of the terrible secret Blake had made me promise to keep.

Then, he did something I'll never understand. Instead of trying to calm the situation or change the subject, he went mad, not just a bit loopy but proper crazy, shouting and telling Dad he had never met a kid like me, that I had no manners and it was about time someone taught me a lesson. Dad looked furious and just for a minute I thought he was going to jump the fence and punch him. I couldn't have been more wrong. Dad was in my face, yelling he had brought me up to be polite and to say 'sorry' to Mr Blake. Well, that did it. I lost it.

'Why are you siding with him? He's the rude one, not me.' The words spewed out like vomit.

'You can't believe what she says. She's a liar,' the bastard screamed as he leant over the fence, his arms flailing. I darted backwards.

'Get in,' Dad ordered grabbing my arm tightly, his fingers pressing into my flesh. He marched me into the kitchen and slammed the door. 'What the hell is he talking about?'

I backed up and shook my head, the confidence I had felt moments before, evaporating. There was no way I was going to tell Dad what had gone on.

'Come on, the truth,' he roared, jettisoning a ball of spittle from his mouth. It landed on my upper lip. I didn't dare wipe it away. 'What the hell is Blake talking about? What have you done?'

Already, he was blaming me. How could he? He didn't have a clue what had happened. I was inside out with anger but he was right about one thing; I had to tell him the truth, well some of it, the bits I could bear to say. I didn't want him to think badly of me, although it was hard to imagine how much lower I could sink in his mind. The only way I could get through it all was to speak very quickly and stare at my shoes. They were my green and blue tartan sneakers. I'd only had them a few weeks. I can still see the stain on the left toe where I'd spilt some gravy. It had happened the first day I wore them. I had wiped it off with the tea-towel but it had left a great greasy mark. I remember crossing one foot over the other so I couldn't see it as I spoke. Some bits sounded so odd, even to me. I wondered if I was making them up. But I knew I wasn't. How could I be? Everything I had been forced to witness that day had been horribly new to me.

'Look, Susan, look!'

I didn't want to look and I didn't want to see. And he shouldn't have made me. I was a little girl, totally innocent. I knew nothing. It never even occurred to me there was anything to know. Dad was standing over me, waiting. For once he wanted me to talk to him but it was hard to tell Dad. For one thing, I didn't have the words. How could I? I had no idea what I was talking about. Not really, except I knew what Blake had done was wrong, more than that, evil. You get a weird feeling in your tummy, a kind of pain that warns you and tells you to run. Except that day I couldn't run, I was too terrified. Besides, he had made me believe there was no escape. I can't remember what I actually said to Dad or the words I used to describe what had happened. I just know the more I gabbled on, the more agitated Dad became. His hands clenched into white-knuckled fists.

As I was talking I glanced upwards to check his reaction. God knows what I expected him to do. What would any Dad do confronted by such a thing? Cry? Yell? Threaten to kill the bastard? Dad did none of these things. Instead his mouth turned downwards into a disapproving arch. I had never seen him look at me that way before. Not like that. I felt dirty. I pulled my cardigan tightly around me and wrenched my skirt down over my legs. Eventually, he turned his head away which was worse because I couldn't see his face and had no way of knowing what he might do next. I needn't have worried. He didn't do anything. I had seen him get more upset when Mum spilt tea on the living room carpet. Do you remember that time he went berserk, screaming and shouting like she'd stabbed someone?

All I wanted was a big hug and him to tell me it would be okay but there was none of that. He told me it was my fault and then kept on and on about how I should never have gone next door and whatever was I thinking, hadn't he told me enough times never to talk to strangers? There was no point in saying Blake wasn't a stranger; he was Mark and Kevin's Dad, our neighbour, a nice man. Dad had had his say and that was that. No answering back. I never spoke to Dad about it again. Not once.

The next day a big black car drew up outside the house. You could hear it a mile off. I watched from the window as a group of kids appeared from nowhere and crowded round all trying to get a glimpse of who was inside. You never saw cars like that in our road. Come to that, in those days, you rarely saw any cars.

Two people, a man and a woman, both wearing dark suits, got out. Even though they weren't in uniform, it was obvious they were police; there was just something about them, unsmiling, not a hair out of place, the woman's grey perm more helmet than hair. The kids giggled and nudged one another, watching as the couple strode up the path. Before they could knock on the door, Dad had already opened it. The next thing I knew, the woman was in the living room with me, settling herself in Dad's chair, if you please. Dad had announced they were coming that morning. No explanation, just that they needed to talk to me. That was it. No reassuring hug, no kind words, nothing. He did pop his head round the door to ask if the police-woman wanted a cup of tea.

'Thank you, white no sugar,' she replied crisply, propping herself up against his cushion.

I could tell by Dad's face, he wasn't happy about that. He didn't say anything just came back in a few minutes later with her drink in some fancy crockery that didn't quite match. The cup was decorated with roses; the saucer with peonies. Both were pink so I doubt she noticed. Dad had put a Bourbon biscuit on the saucer; I eyed it enviously. With Dad out of the way, I sat on what used to be Mum's chair. She would've killed me if she could have seen me. The woman snapped open her brief-case making me jump and took out a pen and pad. My stomach lurched; surely she wasn't planning on actually writing down what I was going to say? It wasn't the sort of thing you commit to paper. Who would want to read that? No one decent. Her gold nib poised, I noticed a tiny bubble of black ink on the tip. It made a slight splodge as she began to write. She looked at me expectantly.

'You already know what happened. You must do or you wouldn't be here. Why make me go through it all again?' Of course, I didn't say any of that. Instead, I thought it might be best to use my imagination. Making something up being preferable to the awful truth. To my surprise, she downed her tea in one go, without even touching the biscuit. I watched with regret as the cream filling melted a little in the saucer. Unlike

54

the last time the police spoke to me after you'd died, there were no dolls to play with and certainly no drawing pictures. All this woman was interested in were the facts, her surprisingly soft voice, slippery with efficiency as she asked question after embarrassing question.

'Stiff or floppy? Floppy or stiff?'

When she said the word 'stiff' she held up her pen to demonstrate its meaning. Like I didn't know. Thankfully, she did not have an equivalent for 'floppy'. I felt sick.

'Stiff or floppy? Floppy or stiff?'

Wasn't it bad enough the bastard had done what he'd done and made me feel ashamed, like it was my fault, when all along it was his? I know that now. Sadly, knowing is not the same as believing. I know there is no Father Christmas but for my son's sake, I'll go along with it. It's good to get caught up in the magic sometimes. Sorry, Mark, I hope you don't mind me mentioning, Billie, my little boy. I want you to know he hasn't taken your place. Promise.

Sorry, where were we? Oh yes, I was saying it was Blake's fault not mine. I should know; I've been told it enough times. Counsellors are very good with words. Unlike me, they always know what to say.

'He was the adult. You were the child,' seems to be their buzzy little mantra but it doesn't stake up against Dad's blunt: 'I blame you.'

Back then, I was just a frightened little girl embarrassed at having to describe, to a stranger, what the neighbour's penis looked like. You need to understand I wasn't one of those knowing, precocious kids who court danger in search of adventure. Had the same thing happened to the boys at school, I imagine they would've just laughed the whole thing off, seeing it as some sort of exciting sex education session. You probably don't have a clue what I'm talking about, do you Mark? Not unless you've grown up and I can't think you age in heaven. I hope for your sake you don't. Trust me, you stay four; you stay innocent. Just don't judge me, Mark. I'm not bad, dirty, tainted, tarnished. I'm still Susan. I'm still your sister.

After the woman had finished writing, covering page after page with her big loopy handwriting, she gave the pad to me. 'You can read, can't you?' she asked when I refused to meet her gaze. Of course, I knew what it said, every rotten word of it. What did I want to read it for? After a while, she took the statement back, then abandoning her honeyed tones, read it out loud in a big booming voice as if she was on stage. She seemed to enjoy the performance, carefully enunciating every syllable, her diction crisp and clear, projecting her voice as if in a theatre. Dad would have heard everything. I entwined my right leg around my left, like the knotted roots of a tree. When she finished she placed what had become her script on the table. I didn't want to put my name to it but she offered me her pen. With its gold nib and black barrel it was irresistible. At school, I wrote with a pencil or a cheap cartridge pen, nothing like this. It felt smooth and heavy as the black ink flowed effortlessly across the page. Having signed my name, I thrust the pad back at her. The deed was done, gone, nothing to do with me. I just wanted it and that bastard to go away. When she opened the door, Dad almost fell into the room. He showed her and the other officer to the door and I heard the three of them talking in hushed tones in the hall. It was too late for whispering. Nevertheless, I took the opportunity to help myself to the Bourbon biscuit. It tasted soft and stale but I ate it anyway.

Dad didn't believe in talking about things. Back then, that's just how it was. There was none of the getting-it-all-out-on-the-table and picking over the pieces with a therapist, like people do these days. For once, I was glad of Dad's 'shut-up and pretend it never happened' approach. The police left, he told me never to tell anyone and that was that. Not even my school knew. Just as well, can you imagine what Paul Brown would have made of that? It's weird but not telling felt as if I was not being honest with people, like I was telling a lie.

One day, when Dad was at work, and I was having a little nose about like I often did when he went out, looking for things to do with Mum or you, trying to make sense of it all and fill in the gaps, I found a newspaper cutting in his drawer. It was folded up really small and hidden in an old tobacco tin. The whole piece can only have been about two inches square. To my relief, my name, together with the sordid details, had been omitted. I was referred to as simply 'local school girl' but I was pleased to see the bastard had not been afforded the same anonymity. Named and shamed as 'Robert Blake, bus driver' for all to see. When I had finished reading, I carefully refolded the fragile paper along the creases, exactly as I had found it and put it back in the drawer. I never mentioned it to Dad, although in an odd way, I was glad he had kept it. It meant he cared, right? And him telling the police, that was his way of trying to help, wasn't it?

It's odd, I'm an adult now but I still can't shake off the feeling I got that day in Blake's kitchen. I was terrified. He was in total control; I had no say. He got to dictate what went on. Weird isn't it? Inside I'm still the kid who went next-door and got more than she bargained for. Obviously, I never saw Tom and Kevin again. I lost my two best friends just because I asked their Dad if I could climb over the fence. I often wondered what they were told. Not the truth, I bet. I still feel bad about them. I can't help it. Thanks to me, they wouldn't have seen their Dad for a while, years even. Perhaps they discovered what happened and lost contact? I hope not. I wouldn't want that on my conscience.

'Who was responsible for those children?' asked a counsellor I saw a few years ago when I told her how guilty I felt about depriving the kids of their father.

'He was.'

'Yes, he was their father. He was the adult. He's the guilty one. Not you.'

I have to keep reminding myself, Mark. I have to keep telling myself, it was his fault, not mine.

'Is that all?' asked one friend when I told her after one too many wines. 'The poor bloke went to prison for that?'

I wanted to dash my glass in her face. What did she know? How dare she try and belittle what had gone on and make me feel guilty because he was suffering the consequences of his actions. If it had happened to her or her daughter, she'd have viewed things very differently. People love to give you their opinions whether you ask for them or not, Mark.

'Well, I think …' they begin, like they're experts. Unless it's happened to them, trust me, they don't have a clue. It was just another of those things that screwed me up for life, in ways I can't explain.

Blake's house was left to go to rack and ruin after he left which seemed appropriate. It gave me some satisfaction to see how time took control of the place and gave decay a free hand to rot window frames, peel paint and allow weeds to take root in the guttering. Unfortunately, I still had to live next-door. I hated the way our house was attached to his with just a thin wall separating my bedroom from his. It would take more than a few bricks to block out the memories.

Years later, after all the fuss had died down and no-one was interested in me or my story anymore, I spotted someone mooching about in his garden, their head bowed examining the weeds. The brown, speckled dome was just the same, disturbingly smooth but the body was different, more stooped. I hid behind the curtain, my heart fit to burst from my ribcage as I watched him bend to caress a dandelion between his fingers as if it were a prize-winning bloom. Bile rose in my throat and I was forced to swallow it as I grabbed Dad by the arm and dragged him over to the window. He peered out, holding back the curtain briefly before letting it drop.

'Yeah, I spotted him a few moments ago. I called the police. They're on their way. He must've wandered off from the centre and managed to find his way back here. God knows how, I heard he lost the plot years ago.'

Unbidden memories of that day flickered behind my eyes.

'He can't hurt you,' said Dad, sounding caring, just like he had that time he discovered me in the wardrobe.

I wanted to tell him the bastard hurt me every day; the pain, like an open sore.

'Look at him,' scoffed Dad peering out as Blake picked a dandelion clock and blew it. 'Silly sod, doesn't even know what time of day it is.'

As the clouds of seeds spiralled through the air, I began to count. 'One o'clock…two o'clock…' I told myself by the time I got to ten o'clock it would all be over, just like I had that day in his house. 'Three o'clock, four o'clock…'

Blake looked up and very briefly our eyes met. Immediately, I looked away but not before I noted no hint of recognition in his rheumy sunken eyes. No acknowledgment of the harm he had done. I wanted to hurt him, just like he had hurt me. He was close enough to the window. I raised my hand to beat my fist against the glass. It was then I noticed, there was still one seed stubbornly attached to the head of the flower. I looked at my watch. It was ten past ten. That was when it had all begun. Time for me to tell everything he couldn't remember but I could never forget.

CHAPTER SEVEN

I don't know how long that bastard got for what he did but let me tell you, having that dirty little secret holed up in the back of my mind is a life sentence. To this day, I worry what people think. Do they think I'm sullied, soiled, some sort of conduit for evil? You know better than anyone, Mark; I make bad things happen. As for what went on next door, even now, I can't help thinking I asked for it, encouraged it even, I must have. Bet you're thinking that's a screwed up way to think? Well, that's what happens, Mark. That's what life does. Like I keep saying, you're better off out of it.

I thought about joining you - still do sometimes. People say it's not the answer, some even believe it's a sin but the thought of being able to do it, if I really want to, is a comfort. Just knowing I can leave it all behind, eases the pain. It's hard to explain and probably even harder for you to understand. Don't worry, I'd never actually do anything. I can't, not now I've got the baby. It wouldn't be fair. Besides, we both know, I don't have the guts. All the same, sometimes it helps to run through the options. I couldn't take an overdose, not after what happened to you. Once, in the Reading Room, I found an article about a woman who had gone to bed and put a plastic bag over her head. No detail was deemed too personal to report. It was all there, even the bit about her urinating on the mattress. There

61

are other ways, of course, some less deliberate, less obvious. Let's just say I'm not always as careful as I should be. I take shortcuts late at night. I'm familiar with them all, the seedy back alleys and the long, unlit streets. I never know who I'm going to meet but I'm not frightened, just the opposite. If anything should happen, it wouldn't be my fault, not really.

Time. I've got to give it time. That's what they say, isn't it? Apparently, time is a great healer. I just wish it would hurry up and get on with it. Funny, how it races through the good bits but drags through the bad. Perhaps we should mess with time the way it messes with us. Let's rewind.

Thanks to the hours I spent in the library and my love of books, I left school with three 'O' levels which was three more than I thought I'd get. Pulling off two 'A's in English Language and English Literature and a 'B' in Art was quite an achievement considering how much I hated school. Dad was furious I didn't get Maths. God knows why, it was never on the cards. Figures weren't my thing. He knew that. Occasionally, the desire to show off his mental agility overcame his indifference towards me and he would emerge from behind his newspaper to show me quick tricks to work out calculations. The trouble was, he was a bad teacher and I was an even worse pupil. He'd start out all calm, then when I didn't get it straightaway, he'd start shouting and scrawl the equations across the page, pressing his pencil down so hard on the paper, the lead would break. I knew what was coming and would take off, always ending up at the Taylors on the edge of the estate. 'Gypsies,' Dad called them but they weren't travellers. They lived in a proper house, granted not a very nice one. I once spotted a banana skin in their toilet bowl, just floating there. I couldn't go when I saw it and had to wait until I got home. I wondered which one of Mrs Taylor's eight sons had put it there. I suspected the youngest, a dirty little boy who used to mess himself. He was seven, old enough to know better. I'd be sitting on the couch next to him and suddenly there'd be the most terrible stench, the sort that makes your eyes sting. He wouldn't even flinch. Judging by the sly smirk he gave me, I think he was actually rather proud. Obviously, I didn't go to see him; I was fifteen, nearly sixteen, and went for the two eldest lads, Tom and Joe.

I had the hots for Joe. I thought I was in love with him. I adored everything about him, the way his long dark hair curled over his collar and his arrogant swagger. He always wore voluminous trousers that hung on his thin, rangy body. I longed to rip them off and frequently did, in the back room, when his Mum was out. Not that she'd have minded. Rose Taylor was a very broad-minded woman; anyone was welcome in her house provided they weren't the police. What her sons got up to was of no consequence to her. They could do what they wanted provided they stayed loyal to her, which of course they did. She was their Mum; they loved her and I could see why. She was easy-going, made no demands. More importantly, she asked no questions. She wasn't stupid, far from it, and the evidence of what her boys got up to was there for all to see. Tom could afford to buy a brand new car but he didn't work. Never had. Yet, his 'motor' as he called it, was pride and joy. Every Sunday morning, there he was out the front, bucket and chamois leather in hand, cleaning it. I'd watch as he lay his T-shirt clad torso, front down across the bonnet to reach every inch of the windscreen. When the glass was as buffed as he was, he'd slide off the car and wink at me.

'Wanna come for a drive?' he'd ask, emptying the dirty water down the drain and slinging the bucket over the hedge into the front garden before opening the passenger door.

'I don't mind,' I'd reply trying to sound cool but feeling excited to be settling myself into the seat, the leather upholstery cold against the back of my bare legs.

When he drove he kept one hand on the wheel, the other on my knee. He always took me to the same place, a quiet lane down by the river lined with swathes of long grass. Back then, it felt like we were the only people who knew about it, just us and the bees that crawled over the cow parsley. It was the prettiest place I had ever seen. But there was only one beauty spot Tom was interested in. I would lie on the ground, his jumper underneath my head and he would bury his head between my legs. We were both happy. I got my ride and he got his. When it came to looks, he was no great shakes. I'm convinced that was part of the reason he needed the car. He had to have something to offer. At least he tried.

Unlike Joe, who didn't have to try at all being blessed with film star good looks. Most times, he barely noticed me. That was what made him so irresistible. Even when we made love or 'shagged' as he so charmingly called it, on the floor in his Mum's back room, his mind seemed to be on other things and the onus was always on me to keep him interested. It was quite a challenge, one I often felt I had failed as he got up and dressed with the air of a man who had just wasted five minutes of his life. I vowed to do better next time and would turn up at all hours in the hope of proving myself.

Unfortunately, I didn't have a close friend I could swop tips with and just sort of made it up as I went along. Joe always gave the impression he was used to better. I'd once spotted him and some blonde necking on the swings in the park. He sported a love bite like a badge of honour for days after - the ugly port wine stain turning a dull brown before it finally faded, leaving no trace. Often, when I showed up at the house, he would be out and my heart would sink.

'Wanna cup of tea, love?' Mrs Taylor would ask, already putting the kettle on. She always made me one whether I wanted it or not, milk and two sugars. I didn't have the heart to tell her I preferred it black.

I'd force down the tea to be polite and when I'd given up all hope of seeing Joe, the door would open and he'd appear, in all his glory. He'd say 'hello' to his mum before disappearing upstairs without so much as a glance in my direction. Once, I followed him, getting as far as the landing but Ben, the least attractive of all the brothers, whipped out of the bathroom to bar my way. At first I thought he was just messing about but I could see from his expression, he meant business. His breath was rancid with smoke, the residue from a thousand fags. Despite his unsavoury appearance, a face full of acne and nose pixelated by blackheads, he thought he was quite the catch, grabbing me roughly around the waist and pushing me up against the wall, his knee inserted between my thighs, his hand following. I squirmed and pushed him away but it made him tighten his grip all the more.

'You know you want it,' he breathed. 'You love it, I know you do.'

I felt sick. Had Joe and Tom told him about what we got up to? How could they? I went with them both because I loved Joe and liked Tom, I felt sorry for him. Was it so bad to want to make them both happy? He seemed to read my mind.

'Joe and Tom didn't say nothing. They didn't have to. I know what goes on. I watch.' He pointed, first at his eyes then at mine before half laughing, half choking. I hoped he was having some sort of seizure but no such luck. He was simply clearing his throat and spat a ball of phlegm over his shoulder before turning his attention back to me, thrusting his groin into mine.

'Give her one from me!' laughed Joe as he swung past and ran down the stairs, dressed to the nines and reeking of after-shave.

'Joe,' I called after him, unable to believe he hadn't wanted to help me. He must've known what was going on.

I tried to arch away from Ben but he grabbed my arm, twisting it awkwardly behind my back. I let out what I hoped was a scream but was more like a growl.

'What the fuck are you doing to her?' Tom suddenly appeared behind Ben and hauled him off me, punching his brother in the face. Ben stumbled backwards and glanced up at me as if he had been wronged. Without a word, he staggered off to his room, slamming the door behind him. It was impossible to know what Tom was thinking.

'You okay?' he asked.

'Fine,' I replied but I wasn't, not really. I hated the way Ben had assumed I was easy meat, but then again, I was going with two of his brothers at the same time; I could hardly blame him for thinking he could have a go too.

'Shall I run you home?' he asked, his car keys already in his hand. Home via the local beauty spot, I thought.

'No, I'll walk,' I told him, pulling my skirt down and being careful not to catch his eye. I didn't like the way he was looking at me.

'Aren't you staying for your tea, Susan?' called Rose, her face suddenly appearing around the toilet door.

I couldn't believe it. She'd been there all along. She must have heard everything but did and said nothing. See what I mean, Mark? I could have been raped right there in her house and she'd have kept her mouth shut. That woman knew how to survive.

'The motor's just outside,' said Tom, waving his car keys and looking at me in that way of his.

I let myself out. It was a long, lonely walk home that day. I never did go back. Of course, Dad didn't notice the young girl who returned that night was different to the one who had skipped out of the door earlier, her head full of dreams, her heart bursting with love for a boy called Joe who, if he knew her name, never bothered to use it. If only Dad had thought to lower his paper, he might have noticed how broken his little girl was and how she longed for a hug. Perhaps if he'd been more affectionate I wouldn't have gone looking for love in all the wrong places. But, hey, I can't blame him. I must take responsibility for my own actions. That's what they say, Mark.

Without the Taylors, life lacked the frisson I had experienced every time I knocked on their door. Cakes, biscuits and sweets were nothing more than a futile attempt to fill the Joe-shaped hole in my life.

'You're going to have to start giving me some money for bills and for all the bloody food you eat,' was Dad's mantra as I comfort-ate my way through another packet of Bourbons. 'Look at the state of you.'

'Have you looked in the mirror recently?' I wanted to snap back but, of course, I didn't.

He was right; I had put on weight. Exactly how much I had no idea. We didn't have a set of scales at home. Dad had thrown Mum's out after she left. One day, when I was at Woolworth's Pick and Mix buying half pound of chocolate caramels, I noticed the weighing machine. You couldn't miss it – a huge red machine with an enormous face and dial. It didn't 'speak your weight' but it didn't need to, not with that needle, pointing out the extent of your fatness for the whole store to see. I didn't get on it, I didn't dare. It was odd, the bigger I got, the more invisible I became. Some women can carry weight and still look good. Not me. I was just ugly, which meant I attracted less attention from men. I was glad, I never did know how to respond to the wolf whistles and smutty suggestions, unlike some of the girls at school who huddled together, giggling and outdoing each other with their lurid remarks. I think one even kept a score sheet. Those same girls loved to goad me about being fat. The more they berated me, the less inclined I was to do anything about it. Not exactly logical but like I keep saying Mark, life makes no sense.

Hardly surprising, I couldn't wait to leave school and take the first job that came along. I'd spotted an ad for a waitress in the window of a small, run-down bed and breakfast. Not so much a fresh start as a grubby one but it was work and I could live-in. It would get me away from Dad, away from our house with all its dark shadows and most importantly away from next door. The woman who showed me round looked run ragged. She spoke rapidly out of the side of her mouth, repeating everything twice, a roll-up permanently attached to her lower lip.

'How old did you say you were? Eighteen? How old did you say you were? Eighteen?'

I didn't say, she had just assumed.

'You don't look eighteen. You don't look eighteen.'

I was barely seventeen but I went along with it all the same.

'Not expecting, are yer? Not expecting? I can't have you here if...'

'No, I'm not,' I told her, hoping I was telling the truth for once. I hadn't had a period for two months. I thought nothing of it; I'd never been regular. I told myself it was stress. That incident with Ben Taylor had taken its toll. But hearing her ask the question made the possibility I had been ignoring, real. If I was pregnant, it could be Joe or Tom's.

'Okay, okay. Any experience in the hotel trade? Any experience...?'

Before she could repeat herself, I cut in, 'Yes, I've done waitressing and cleaning.' I was getting good at lying. Too good, even I believed it.

She squinted through the smoke, scrutinizing me, deciding whether I passed muster.

'I'll work for free for a week. If you don't like me, I'll leave.'

It was too good an offer for her not to take. She looked around at the shabby hall and stairwell with its chipped paint, unable to conceal her amazement that anyone would want to work there for money, let alone for nothing. She drew long and hard on her cigarette, holding the ever-decreasing white stump between her thumb and forefinger, before plucking it from her lips and emitting a puff of smoke that enveloped her face.

'You mad? You mad?' She laughed, a life-threatening, double-barrelled choke. 'Wanna see the room?'

Before she could ask again, I nodded and followed her up the uncarpeted stairs to the third floor. The walls were papered in the cheapest woodchip and covered in black scuff marks where people had obviously brushed past carelessly with their luggage. She opened the door onto a bedroom that was just that, a bed in a room. Nothing more. No chair, no wardrobe, not even a chest of drawers. It was obvious the space should have been much bigger but had been partitioned off. What remained was little more than a box. The only original feature it retained was a Victorian sash window, making the room appear larger than it really was.

'Job's yours if you want it.'

I didn't need telling twice, and went home to pack a bag, wrapping the framed photo of you that Mum had taken, in a shirt. You were about eighteen months at the most, and you were sitting on the grass in the back garden with your arms outstretched. Mum loved that picture, kissing it every night before she went to sleep. I used to hover in the doorway, watching, hoping she'd call me in for a cuddle. I often wondered why she didn't take that photo with her when she left. It was only small and would've easily fitted inside her handbag, in that little pocket where she kept her compact and lipstick.

Much to my relief, Dad wasn't there when I left home but I knew he'd be relieved I'd gone. All the same, I thought I should let him know where I was going and tore the corner off his newspaper, wrote down the address of the B&B and left it, propped up on the mantelpiece.

Just for the record, Mark, if I was pregnant, he was the last person I'd tell.

CHAPTER EIGHT

Mrs Reynolds as she insisted I call her, was delighted to have another pair of hands to clean toilets, change sheets and do the seemingly endless piles of laundry that running a bed and breakfast entailed. For a while, I enjoyed being there. I really did. The work was tiring but mindless. I liked that. It meant I didn't have to think about anything. Not even you. For the first few days, Mrs Reynolds followed me about, getting on my nerves, checking up on me but once she knew she could trust me to do things properly, we got along just fine.

'I don't have to ask you twice. I don't have to ask you twice,' she'd say, enjoying her little joke.

The week's free trial passed without incident and the following Monday I started work for real. We divided the tasks between us according to what we enjoyed the most. She cooked. I cleaned. I've got a touch of OCD. It means I like things to be neat and tidy. Very neat and tidy. What some people might regard as an affliction was an asset at the B&B. I had the place organised in no time: rooms were ready by eleven for receiving guests at twelve and the dining room was always spotless, the tables polished and laid with gleaming cutlery and glasses. Mrs Reynolds was delighted with my work, if not my appearance.

'You're not, are you? Are you?'

My belly had swollen to fill the space between us. I shook my head but in truth, I had no idea. There was a chance but not one I was prepared to consider.

'You can't stay here if you are. You'll have to go. I'll need your room for someone who can do the work.'

'I'm not pregnant,' I snapped. 'It's all those fried breakfasts you keep feeding me.'

She needn't have worried. That evening, I miscarried. I stayed in bed all the next day. It wasn't the pain so much as the shock. I'd convinced myself I wasn't pregnant only to discover I was and I wasn't in the very same moment. I didn't leave my room for two days, telling Mrs Reynolds I had period pain. It wasn't a lie, not really - it amounted to the same thing. No baby. I bundled the bloody sheets into a refuse sack and hid it underneath my bed, vowing to buy a replacement set of linen when I got paid.

'You alright? You alright?' she asked suspiciously when I eventually appeared in the dining room.

'Fine, thanks.'

The thought of a day's work, with all the lifting and carrying it involved was daunting. The dining room hadn't been touched in two days and to me, looked filthy. Guests couldn't be expected to eat there. I filled a bucket with water and stupidly attempted to lift it out of the sink. It was too heavy and I dropped it. Mrs Reynolds ran over.

'Leave it. Sit down. You look terrible. You look terrible. Here, have a drink.' She took a glass from the cupboard, filled it with water, then held it to my lips. 'Slowly, sip it slowly. Go back to bed. We're not busy. I can cope down here.' She helped me to my room.

'Thanks, I'll be okay,' I murmured, but she insisted on putting me to bed and, before I could stop her, pulled back the covers to reveal the blood-stained mattress. To her credit, she didn't flinch. She must've guessed what had happened but she wasn't about to embarrass me. She simply left the room, returned with some fresh linen and without a word, made up the bed. I got in gratefully and lay down, the tears balancing on my cheeks before falling onto the pillow. It was Mrs Reynolds' fault; she had been kind and I couldn't deal with that. Had she been angry or disappointed I could have coped. The funny thing was I wasn't crying for my lost baby, I was crying for you but I couldn't tell her. I wouldn't have known where to begin. She pulled the counterpane up and rested her hand on my forehead.

'You ain't got a temperature; you'll live. I'll call the doctor out if needs be. Now get some sleep. If you want anything, anything at all, just shout.'

A few months later, Mrs Reynolds noted brightly 'Bookings are up.' She was perusing the diary, running her yellowing index finger down the long list of entries written in her indecipherable hand. 'That Mr Liddle has been in for his dinner more or less every night for the past three weeks. Not offering extras on the side, are you?'

'No, of course not.' I could feel my cheeks colour. I wasn't in the mood for jokes. Losing the baby had left me bereft. In some ways, it made no sense; I was grieving for someone I had never met, never known. I didn't want a baby but when it was taken from me, I wanted it more than anything in the world. For a while, I blamed myself. What was wrong with my body? I didn't feel like a woman, not a real one. After all, my body had rejected and killed my baby. Meanwhile, Mrs Reynolds tried to jolly me along. People do that a lot, Mark. Don't ask me why. It makes no sense.

'I'm only joking. I'm only joking but let's face it, Mr Liddle's not here for my cooking.' She was right there. Her culinary skills were not up to much although her eggs and bacon were unforgettable, repeating on me for days.

'I've seen him. I've seen him. Can't take his eyes off you. He's posh. Nicely spoken. Here, wanna fag? Wanna fag?' She offered me the roll-up she'd just made. Having watched her furry, rubbery tongue lick the cigarette paper it was easy to decline. She put it in her mouth, where it stayed unlit, glued to her lower lip. 'Mark my words, he likes you.'

What did I care? I was off men. Ben and Joe Taylor had seen to that. Losing the baby was the price I paid for going with the pair of them. My body, unable to tell the difference between miscarrying a much longed-for baby or losing a life unplanned, made sure I suffered. I took to staying in bed a lot. When I wasn't working, I slept. If only I could have slept through my dreams. Each night was a hellish trip into the past. When I awoke, panic-stricken, I kept the curtains closed, unable to look out at people, happily going about their lives, perfect mums with perfect husbands and perfect kids.

My partner doesn't know any of this. Did I mention I had a boyfriend? No, I don't think I did. I've been so intent on trying to explain everything and make sense of the past I haven't told you what's happening now. I am Mrs Liddle, well as good as. I live with our best customer, Liam. Mrs Reynolds was right; he did like me. He liked me enough to eat in our dining room every night and suffer her liver and onions. He liked me enough to fight my corner.

It was one night, just before Christmas. I was still feeling low but it was one of our busiest times of the year so I had to get on with it. Blinded by pound signs, Mrs Reynolds had taken the biggest booking of her life and, for one night only, had filled every room in the boarding house with a party of office workers on the razz. Presumably their budget didn't stretch to the more salubrious hotels but they wanted to make a night of it and the B&B afforded them that opportunity. Although they planned to do the bulk of their celebrating at the local nightclub, they had requested an evening meal on arrival, presumably to line their stomachs in preparation for the revelry ahead. Mrs Reynolds, spotting a rare opportunity to make a tidy profit, had rashly agreed what she loosely termed a 'festive menu' of soup, chicken and fruit salad. In an attempt to perk up the dingy dining room and create something of a party atmosphere, she had nipped to the corner shop and bought crackers, balloons and party poppers to add some much-needed Christmas cheer. I remember the pair of us spent a surprisingly happy afternoon decorating the room as she reminisced.

'Every year, Mum and me used to spend hours making paper chains. What a waste of bloody time!' I liked Mrs Reynolds. I knew where I stood with her.

That night, she insisted on me wearing a black skirt and white blouse for the occasion and lent me her old uniform from her silver service days. The skirt was far too big and I had to use a safety pin to secure the waistband.

'Oh my God! You can't go out there looking like that. You'll frighten the punters. Here, put this on,' she said, taking off her cardigan and handing it to me. Reluctantly, I put it on. It reeked of chips and cigarettes.

Already drunk when they checked-in late on Friday evening, some of the group took exception when they discovered a handful of other diners would be eating with them, complaining they had made an exclusive booking.

'I've done you a special deal. I've done you a special deal. Them's our regulars. It's Christmas, I can't turn them away, can I?' Mrs Reynolds said, gesturing to Liam and a young couple holding hands at the corner table. She winked at me and I could tell she enjoyed her sly 'no room at the inn,' biblical reference, a joke that was lost on the well-oiled office manager who immediately demanded the other diners be ejected.

'It's Christmas, the more the merrier. Enjoy yourselves. I'm sure you've earned it. I'm sure you've earned it,' she told him, picking up a Christmas cracker and thrusting one end at him, giving him little option but to pull it. With a green paper hat on his head, he lost all credibility and sat down.

Fortunately, no one knew or cared the food was processed, straight out of packets and tins, although the near perfect circular slices of chicken should have been a giveaway. Some made a half-hearted attempt to eat what was put in front of them but most pushed it to one side, in favour of the wine, a bottle of red and white set out on each table.

'Oi, grandma, over here,' shouted a man, leaning back in his chair to grab Mrs Reynolds by the elbow as she passed, causing her to spill the two bowls of soup she was carrying.

'Your wine is on the table,' she replied steadily.

'We paid for a bottle each. Where's the rest of our booze, old lady?'

Mrs Reynolds looked hurt. It was a pitiful sight. For a moment I thought she might cry, either that or dash the plates she was carrying into the side of his head. To my surprise, she did neither, just stood there and sort of crumpled, doubled over like a used tissue.

'You've had our money, where's our wine? You and Cinders drank it all, eh?' He turned to look at me. 'Bet you don't eat this muck. You don't eat anything by the look of you, you bag of bones.'

It made a change from being called 'fat' but, even so, it wasn't nice. The girl to his left sniggered. I felt like crying, what with all the other women dolled up and me standing there in Mrs Reynolds' ugly over-sized waitress uniform. Liam went over to the man and whispered something in his ear before taking him by the arm and steering him across the restaurant and out through the front door. A small contingent started to bang the tables with their fists, saying the place was a 'dump' and the food 'shit'. Someone even flung a piece of chicken roll, Frisby-style across the room at Liam when he came back in. He calmly bent down, picked it up and put it back on the man's plate. Then, he went to his table and raised his glass.

'Merry Christmas. Now, I think it's time the rest of you took the party elsewhere.' With that, he sat down and drained his glass. I could have kissed him.

The group had had their fill and were more than happy to head off. When the last of the stragglers had gone, Liam persuaded Mrs Reynolds to get some rest and helped me clear away.

'Thanks for what you said earlier. Not many people would have done that,' I told him, handing him a stack of dirty plates to load into the dishwasher.

'The guy was drunk. He'll wake up with a hangover and not remember a thing,' he smiled. 'Although I daresay the food might repeat on him.'

'If it's so bad, why d'you keep coming?' His well-cut suit and expensive-looking shoes suggested he was used to far better. 'Seriously, it's not exactly five star, is it?'

'You really need me to tell you? I come for you.' He burped loudly. 'Sorry that was the stuffing.' For the first time in I don't know how long, I laughed. 'There's nothing for it,' he said. 'You'll just have to go out with me.'

'Why?' I asked, delighted.

'Because I can't keep coming here and eating her food.' He lifted up his jumper to reveal his potbelly.

A year later and I had only just recognised what he was offering: love, undiluted and unconditional. Sadly, it didn't take long before my suspicious mind got to work. One time he bought me a bottle of very expensive perfume for no apparent reason and I accused him of having an affair. At the time, it made perfect sense. If I wore the same scent as his mistress I wouldn't suspect him of being unfaithful if I caught a whiff of Chanel on his clothes. As always, Liam was calm and patient, never once turning on me for thinking the worst of him. Thankfully, my paranoid fantasies never became a reality and gradually, I began to trust him. Yet, I was never truthful with him, not completely. He didn't need to know about the miscarriage and I didn't want to tell him about the Taylors. Why risk spoiling everything?

CHAPTER NINE

'A baby?' I repeated, when Liam told me his heart's desire.

I had never wanted a child. Women aren't supposed to think like that but after what had happened to you, how could I risk it? It never even occurred to me Liam might have other ideas.

'But we haven't known each other long and we're not married, not even engaged,' I said lamely, as if any of that mattered. 'Don't you want to marry me?' Unlike most girls, I wasn't bothered about a ring, I just wanted Liam to propose. That way I would know he cared enough to ask.

'I thought we were talking about having a baby, not getting married,' he replied.

'You're the one talking about having a baby, not me.'

'Don't you want kids?' I could tell by his tone he was shocked. I might not be as keen as he was on years of broken sleep and guilt but I didn't want to lose him. He was my rock. I needed him.

'Is it a deal-breaker?' I asked, dreading the answer. What should have been a joyful conversation had taken a dark turn.

'Deal-breaker? Sorry, I just assumed you'd want a family.'

'I'm happy, just you and me. I love it. I love you.'

79

'I'm happy, very happy. That's why … oh forget it, I'm being selfish.'

'No you're not. There's nothing selfish about wanting a baby. You're allowed to say what you'd like.'

'Yes, but if it's not what you want...' He trailed off, hoping I might leap in and fill the gap. 'You don't want kids then.'

Liam meant it as a statement but it sounded like more of a question. One I wasn't ready to answer. He waited a while before landing the big one on me. He must have known it was his trump card but I don't think he played it intentionally; he wasn't the manipulative type.

'Being adopted means I've never had a blood link with anyone. A kid of my own would be a dream come true.' I knew he was adopted but had no idea it was such a huge deal. It never even crossed my mind it might impact on me one day. 'Mum died last year. It would mean so much to have my own child, my own flesh and blood.'

Bang! He'd done it. How could I argue with that? He had often told me about how he had never met his birth mother, how he had never wanted to look for her for fear of upsetting his Mum. All credit to the woman, she'd done a great job. Patient, kind and loving, Liam would make a wonderful father. My worry was what sort of a mother I would be. It wasn't fair on the child or Liam. I couldn't risk it even if it did mean losing him.

'I'm not sure I can have children.' It wasn't a lie. Given the miscarriage I may well have had difficulty keeping a baby to full term. Of course, I should have just told him the truth, 'I'm not sure I want children.'

'What makes you think you can't have kids?'

80

'I've always had problems. Women's stuff,' I said, hating myself for compounding the lie.

'But if you could, you'd like a baby? Our baby?'

No one had ever wanted anything that big from me, not even you, and you had been one hell of a responsibility, Mark. It wasn't your fault, I'm just saying. It was too much. Mum and Dad just assumed looking after you was my job, not theirs. And look what happened.

The Taylors had taken what they wanted. We made love but there was no love on their part.

Now here was a man who thought the world of me. A man I trusted. A man I loved and who loved and respected me, yet I couldn't bring myself to give him the one thing he wanted the most. How could I after what had happened to you? A baby was a big ask and just because I was his girlfriend didn't mean I had to go along with it. All the same, I wanted to make him happy. I owed him that. If I didn't give him a baby no one else would, not as long as we were together and I didn't want to lose him.

'We'd better start trying then,' I told him, convinced fate would intervene and punish me by ensuring I could not conceive.

You had died in my care. I wasn't fit to look after a child. I'd proved that. I'd had one miscarriage and was sure I'd read it could make getting pregnant again less likely. My cycle was erratic which wasn't a good sign either. No, there was no chance of me getting pregnant.

We all like to think we're in control; it's the only way to cope. Trouble is, when a curved ball hits, it upends you. Trying for a baby was more than a gamble, it was madness. If I'd given it a moment's thought I'd never have gone along with it, let alone stopped taking the Pill. I don't know what possessed me. I convinced myself it was nothing more than a harmless game of Russian roulette, where the odds of conceiving were stacked against me.

The pain came on suddenly the night after Liam left to go on yet another training course. He was a successful marketing manager and his company was keen for him to keep abreast of the latest skills. Even if he had been with me, there was nothing he could have done. I slept most of the time and in the fleeting moments I was conscious, I felt worse than ever, dragging myself to the loo where I was violently ill. Eventually I managed to call the doctor, pleading for a home visit. When the GP arrived, he seemed annoyed to have been called out for something he considered minor. After a brief examination and a few cursory questions, he fobbed me off with some Penicillin and anti-sickness tablets.

By the time Liam came home, a few days later, I was in a terrible state. In and out of sleep I had lost all track of time. When the week was up, I had finished the medication but still showed no signs of recovery.

'I'll make you an appointment at the surgery. I'll take time off and come with you,' said Liam. 'In the meantime, I got you this, some herbal stuff. The woman in the chemist said it's good for sickness.'

Weak and frail, I was happy to try anything and readily downed the two lozenge-shaped tablets he gave me. The next day, I felt like I was dying, I couldn't face getting into a car, let alone a drive to the surgery but Liam looked worried so I agreed to go, clutching a plastic bag the whole journey just in case.

An elderly, blunt, no-nonsense sort, it was easy to see why Dr Pearce was the least popular and therefore the least busy of the four practitioners at the surgery. The receptionist had had no trouble slotting me into her empty diary. The woman was old school and gave me a thorough examination, asking a volley of probing questions before removing her stethoscope and placing it on the desk. She sat and looked at me, her hands clasped together in her lap. Why wasn't she reaching for her pad and pen to write me a new prescription?

'If I could just have some stronger antibiotics, I'll be fine,' I implored, desperate to get back to bed and lie down.

'I'm not giving you any more drugs until I've done a pregnancy test.'

'But I can't be pregnant,' I exclaimed, feeling sicker than ever. 'We only did it once.' I knew it was nonsense but she had just suggested something even more ridiculous.

'Once is enough,' she replied. I could tell by the way she rolled her eyes she was exasperated with me.

'You could be, love,' Liam said, practically levitating with joy. 'You might be expecting our baby. Oh my God, my love. I love you.' He leapt up to embrace me but the doctor intervened.

'Take this,' she said, handing me a small glass bottle. 'Can you manage a sample? Just a drop will do, then I can send it to the lab. That way we'll soon know for sure.'

We'd gone from me having some sort of infection to a pregnancy test in two minutes. Convinced she was wrong, I took the bottle and made my way unsteadily to the loo. The sooner we eliminated this baby nonsense, the sooner she could investigate the real cause and find a cure.

Liam was all for buying a pregnancy test at the chemist to avoid the wait but the doctor's results would be more reliable. Besides I couldn't see the point in wasting money. I wasn't pregnant and that was that.

'You're pregnant,' said the doctor when I snuck in to see her two days later while Liam was at work. At first, I couldn't speak, hoping if I didn't acknowledge it, it would cease to be real.

She handed me a tissue and then another and another but no amount was sufficient to stem the tears. I don't remember crying as much before but I've cried plenty since, believe me.

'You don't seem very happy, Susan. Do you want this baby?' What a question to have to ask and an even worse one to answer. I didn't want the baby, of course I didn't. I didn't trust myself. But I didn't want the alternative either.

'Take your time. Think about it, Susan. You don't have to make any decisions right now.'

I didn't like the way she kept using my name, putting the onus directly on me, making whatever happened my fault. I was crying harder now, like a kid when it falls over and all hell breaks loose.

'You don't have to keep it; you know that. There are things we can do.'

I couldn't believe what I was hearing. I resented her assumption. It was too fast, too off pat and, in my opinion, unprofessional. 'No,' I told her, blowing my nose. 'I don't want an …'

Before I could say the word she thrust another box of tissues at me. 'Here, take them. Go home, calm down and think about it very carefully. Weigh up the pros and cons. Make the decision for you, no-one else.'

I knew she meant Liam but she didn't understand. How could she? She wore expensive clothes and had letters after her name. I bet her Mum didn't chain smoke or lock her in a wardrobe.

'When you're ready, come back and let me know what you've decided. There's plenty of time – you're only about six weeks. Do what's right for you, Susan. If you're not ready, you can ...'

I didn't want to hear anymore of what she had to say. It was my body, my baby. Out of nowhere I suddenly felt a connection.

'I'm keeping this baby.'

'You've had a shock, why don't you make another appointment for a week's time and we can talk about it again? You really ought to.' I could see her mouth moving but I couldn't hear a word she was saying. My stomach lurched and I thought I was going to vomit right there on the floor in front of her.

'Oh my God. What about all the stuff I've taken? My God, no! What have I done?'

'The medication we gave you? Don't worry. Let me see, you've had two types of antibiotics. I'll double-check but they should be fine. I've prescribed them to my pregnant patients before.' With that, she reached for her pharmaceutical directory, flicking through the well-thumbed pages until she found the entry she was looking for. It was a process that seemed to take forever. Had I had the strength I would've wrenched the book from her and done it myself. 'Ah, here we are,' she said, reading to herself, silently and very, very slowly.

Eventually, she looked up and smiled in what she clearly hoped was a reassuring manner. 'Yes, as I thought. All fine. No worries. Obviously, we can't say for sure, but your baby is very well protected in there. The chances are you'll both be fine.

Now, promise me you'll try to relax. Stress isn't good for you in your condition.'

Already it was all about the baby. I had been ill for weeks. No one cared. Then a baby comes along and suddenly it's a big deal. My annoyance was soon replaced by anxiety. How could I have been so stupid? The doctor must have recognised the panic on my face.

'You haven't taken anything else, have you?'

I nodded, ashamed and worried beyond belief.

'Just some herbal stuff; the antibiotics weren't working. I'm so sorry.'

'What was it? Can you remember?'

I was shaking, desperately trying to picture the label, the logo, anything. It was no use, I couldn't think, my mind was too preoccupied with the possible horrific consequences of my actions.

'I've still got the stuff indoors. I'll ring you with the name as soon as I get back.'

The receptionist called me a cab and I arrived at Liam's in record time. On his suggestion, I had moved in a few weeks before, much to Mrs Reynolds' annoyance, losing not only her best-ever char but also her best friend. Despite Liam doing everything to make me feel welcome, the place didn't feel like home. Don't ask me why. It was too modern, too designer, too good for me. I went straight to the bathroom cabinet and opened it. There was the bottle, its label facing me. *Melatonin.* What the hell was it? I had just taken it, without asking any questions, on trust. What a fool. I scanned the label. Nothing. Then I found the box and read the information sheet, twice, three times, four maybe just to make sure. Then I spotted it. How had I missed it? The bit about pregnant women and nursing mothers needing to consult their GP before taking it was right there in bold type. I rang the doctor immediately and told her. She was sure *Melatonin* was harmless but, hearing the fear in my voice, she double-checked leaving me hanging on, imagining the worst.

'Don't worry. Obviously, it's best to avoid taking any drugs you don't absolutely need when you're pregnant, especially over-the-counter medication but from what I've read you and the baby should be okay. Obviously, I can't say for definite. Later, we can run some tests but ...'

Oh God. I just wanted a straight 'Yes, your baby will be fine.' No matter how much I pleaded and begged, she remained on the fence. Looking back I realise she had no option but at the time her attitude left me nowhere to go but hell. And that's where I stayed for the duration of my pregnancy. It didn't matter how much Liam reassured me or how elated he was when scans and tests were fine. No, I had to torment myself, reading and rereading anything and everything I could find about the wretched drug. I even went so far as to telephone the manufacturer.

'It's safe. Trust me. If my wife was pregnant, I'd tell her to take it. In fact, it's so efficacious, I'd insist,' the over-confident young man on the other end of the phone assured me. He probably wasn't even married.

'Is your wife pregnant?'

'No, but if she was I ...'

I hung up. No one was taking the threat to this baby seriously. I felt like I had tried to sabotage a life before it had even begun. What was wrong with me? I started thinking it might be best to terminate. No baby would want me as a mother. You know that, Mark. Better than anyone.

Liam felt no guilt at having given me the tablets and, as he kept reminding me, the baby would be fine. The doctor had said so and even the manufacturer had been willing to go out on a limb. To him, it was all a matter of logic but I didn't care what anyone said because no one knew for sure what harm may have been done until the baby was born. I may not have wanted a baby but I never wanted this. 'I'm sorry,' I whispered to my belly, not even daring to stroke it. 'I didn't know.'

I didn't like being pregnant. Some women do. They bloom. They blossom. I was sick for what felt like months. On the rare occasions I could face food, I couldn't eat without getting heartburn. Every check-up, every scan left me riddled with insecurity. My GP, knowing how worried I was about having taken the medication signed me up for a battery of tests. Far from quelling my anxiety, I worried incessantly as I anticipated the worst.

'God, pregnancy don't suit you, does it?' Mrs Reynolds said when she visited. 'Never mind, just a few more days to go, eh? Have they said what you're having?'

'A boy.'

She smiled wistfully. 'I knew it. Got a name yet? Arthur's nice. I like Arthur.'

'No, no name.'

'Oh, well, as soon as that baby comes you'll know. You'll say, 'He looks just like an Arthur.''

I didn't dare give him a name, just in case.

She eyed up the acres of baby paraphernalia littering the living room: piles of tiny blue clothes, packs of nappies stacked against the wall like breeze blocks, a top of the range pram that looked like it cost more than a new car, a cot complete with canopy and enough toys to keep every kid in the neighbourhood happy.

'He's going to be quite the little prince,' she noted.

'No, he's not,' I snapped.

She looked taken aback. 'Right, well must get on… got a big party booked this weekend. Just wanted to pop by to see how you were getting on.'

Before I realised what she was doing, she bent down, placed her palm on my bump and rubbed it softly. 'You'll be fine, little one. Have a wonderful life,' she whispered into my belly button.

In a single, simple gesture she had made a connection with my baby, more than I had managed to achieve in almost nine months. She turned to me. 'You alright?'

She knew I wasn't but I couldn't bring myself to tell her about the drugs I'd taken. It didn't matter how reassuring the doctor had been, I was still worried, and I had no intention of telling her what had happened to you, although in a funny way, I think she would've understood. I gave her a nod and she knew me well enough not to pursue it, leaving with a wave of her hand.

'Anything you need. You know where I am. In the meantime, don't worry. You'll be fine.'

How could she say that? She had no idea but she was right about the baby being a little prince in the making. Liam's job paid well but even so I couldn't justify the money he lavished on our unborn child, especially not when I thought about how little we had as kids. My belief about you being 'the Golden Child' was childish. In truth you weren't treated any differently to me, not really. Money was just as scarce when you arrived.

Yet here was Liam over-indulging a son he didn't have. Not yet. It was tempting fate.

'Put all this stuff in the garage,' I told him when he turned up with another armful.

'Don't be daft, Baby will be here soon.'

'Stick the lot outside or I'll take it back to the shop myself. And for God's sake stop calling him Baby.'

He tried to hold me but I pulled away. It was letting him get close that had got me in this mess. I wanted to run away but I couldn't move, I was too full of Baby.

Even today, I find it hard to talk about the birth. Let's just say it was difficult. The build-up had been bad enough with Liam counting down the days to the birth, like a kid at Christmas. The final straw came when he bought a video camera to film all the gory details. It felt like the ultimate intrusion. More importantly, why record something that had the potential to go wrong? He wasn't happy with my decision to go it alone but respected my wishes.

During the sixteen-hour labour, I was awash with pethidine and whatever other drugs they had pumped into me when they stuck the epidural in my spine.

My baby was born into chaos. A theatre full of medics chatted and laughed as they wielded scalpels to cut him free of me, producing a baby, like masked magicians, from behind the green screen erected across my belly. But there was no applause at this side show. He was not handed to me to hold but was whisked away. No kiss, no love, just a cursory glimpse of his head. He could have been any baby; perhaps the staff had one on standby. If there's ever an optimum time to bond with your child, that's it, the moment they're born. Once you've filled their heart with love, nothing and no one can change that.

I didn't get to meet my baby for two days. He was too ill. Nothing serious, the nurse assured me, he just needed help with his breathing. I wasn't to worry.

During that lost time, I slept, I dreamt, I wet the bed. The nurse took forever to change the sheets, muttering underneath her breath as I watched her unfold the crisp white linen and shake it out over the mattress, just as I had done so many times at the B&B. I felt guilty for making her more work but what could I do, an arm attached to a drip, a needle in the back of my hand?

'How is my baby? Can I see him?' I asked whenever anyone in a uniform walked past, hoping someone would be kind enough to break rank and bring him to me. My request was usually greeted by a sympathetic smile from a kindly nurse or a look of utter bewilderment from a woman I later discovered to be a cleaner. High on painkillers and with no baby in the cot beside my bed, I began to wonder if I'd actually given birth.

When Liam came to visit, he was the happiest I'd ever seen him. Having gone to Special Care to meet his son, he went into raptures about his beautiful boy, so small in his vast incubator, tubes snaking about him, keeping him alive. I didn't want to listen. It was too painful. I turned away and began to cry. Silent tears I didn't want him to see.

'Okay, Sue. I'll let you get some rest. See you later. I love you so much. Wait 'til you see him. He'll make you feel like you've never felt before.'

He was right there.

'Okay, bye, get some sleep. I'm nipping down to see my son again. I love saying that, 'my son'.'

Already the baby was 'his' son, not 'ours'.

'I'll tell him Mummy sends her love,' he smiled proudly as he kissed me goodbye.

It was odd being referred to as 'Mummy'. I was no longer just Susan; I was a mum with another person dependent on me. That was going to take some getting used to.

I was glad Liam wasn't there when a nurse appeared from behind the curtain with the baby in her arms. She placed him on my chest as if she was setting down a plate of toast. Before I could lift my hand to hold him steady, he slipped to one side and landed like a fledgling on the covers beside me.

'Can we take the drip out so I can hold him?'

She shook her head and picked him up, putting him face down on my breast.

'What are you doing?' I asked alarmed, unprepared.

'It says on your notes you want to breast-feed, yeah?'

The casual 'yeah' annoyed me.

'No, yes, but I'm sore everywhere and I don't know how to do it.'

It was embarrassing having to admit that unlike the other women on the ward who nursed their babies night and day, motherhood did not come naturally to me. I can still hear the nurse laughing now, a mocking snort emitted from her piggy snout. 'You don't know but he does.'

If he did, he wasn't letting on as all my attempts to get him to feed failed. There was no reason, it just wasn't happening. The nurse huffed and puffed, making me feel even more of a freak for not being able to do something that should have come naturally. Eventually, she had no option but to lift him off and place him in his see-through Perspex cot. He peered at me with huge eyes, his puny arms poking out of the gaping holes in his sleep-suit and his hands scrunched into small, useless fists. Occasionally, he would unfurl his fingers and reach out to me. What did he want? I felt drained. I had nothing to give but could tell from the determined way he held my gaze he would never let me go.

When the drip came out and the drugs wore off, I finally held him for the first time. I liked the way he felt, all warm and he fitted snugly into the crook of my arm just like you had done the day Mum brought you home from hospital. Dad had told me you'd be arriving that morning and I had stayed awake all the previous night, too excited to sleep.

'Take him, he won't bite,' she had told me, a half-smoked cigarette stuck to her bottom lip.

At first, I'd enjoyed the warmth of you and the way you sucked my little finger as a comforter but years later it was obvious Mum was training me for the years of baby-minding ahead. The more she expected of me, the more frightened I became of the screaming woollen bundle that stank of cheese and rabbit droppings. I'm sorry, Mark, it wasn't your fault. You were only a baby but I was only a child. You were not my responsibility unlike this screaming, red-faced bundle demanding I go to him. As I shifted gingerly across the bed, careful not to pull my stitches, the pain from my scar took me by surprise. I gasped, feeling like I had a sack of potatoes stapled to my pubic bone. Slowly, I eased myself from under the stiff cotton sheets and carefully swung my legs over the side of the bed. The floor felt cold and sticky against the soles of my bare feet. Suddenly woozy, I lurched forwards, steadying myself on the side of the cot. My baby looked at me, mentally circling me. Neither of us smiled. I could see by the way he screwed up his eyes before turning his head away, he was unhappy with me. And who could blame him? He'd not exactly lucked out with me for a mum. He yawned. Clearly, I already bored him.

'What are you doing out of bed?' asked a nurse, suddenly drawing back the curtain to reveal me, and all my inadequacies to the ward. 'Have you tried feeding him today?'

I shook my head, defeated.

'You must give it a go. He must be hungry.'

Doing as I was told, I sat back, wincing as a sudden pain across my belly caught me unawares. Without asking, the nurse undid the first three buttons of my top before lifting the baby out of his cot and dumping him face down on my chest, repositioning baby and breast until they were perfectly aligned. The baby snuffled, his silky head bobbing up and down.

'Here darling, this way,' she said, gently guiding his head in the right direction.

He latched on. The pain was unbearable, I jumped, the baby slipped and began to wail. Annoyed, the nurse grabbed my breast in her hand and guided my nipple missile-like into his mouth. He sucked for a moment then lost interest. The nurse repeated the same performance on the other side. He squirmed away, clearly horrified at being confronted by a nipple the size of his fist.

'You could at least try,' she snapped.

'Yes, he could.'

'I meant you, not the baby,' she scolded replacing him in his cot. 'I'll be back in a moment to give it another go.' She walked away, going to close the curtain then changing her mind and leaving me, the failure of a mother, for all to see.

The woman in the bed opposite was smiling, yet her newborn's incessant crying filled the ward. Why couldn't I be like her, calm and patient? My boy had been saddled with a dud. Even he could see the other women mothering their offspring like they were born to it. I know what you're thinking Mark, and I don't blame you. But you're wrong. Somewhere deep inside me, in a place I couldn't quite reach, was a well of love for my baby. He meant more to me than you. That was part of the problem. I had loved you and look what had happened. I couldn't risk getting close to him, could I? Sometimes, I would see him lying in his cot, so small and I'd sneak him into my bed.

'Where's Baby?' the nurse would ask, as if I'd eaten him.

Proudly, I pulled back the sheet to reveal you snuggled beside me.

'No, we don't do that here!' she would cry, plucking him out of his nest. 'You'll smother him in your sleep!'

Why did she say that? What did she know? Had she already marked me out as a danger to my child? Perhaps she could see something, sense the signs?

Thanks to the brutal Caesarean, my baby had been wrenched from my body, amid so much bloodshed; it felt like we'd been at war since the day he was born.

I couldn't bring myself to tell Liam how I felt. The man was delirious with joy, showering us with gifts, chocolates for me, trinkets for the baby, covering my bedside cabinet and the seat of the ugly plastic visitors' chair.

'How about Lee?' he'd asked one morning, having arrived bright and early like he always did.

'Lee?'

'Lee Liddle. Sounds good to me.'

'Sounds like Pee Piddle.'

He looked at me and we laughed. Or at least I think we did. It had been so long since I'd even smiled, I'm not sure I'd recognised happiness anymore.

'Here, have a chocolate,' he said, lifting the lid on the box and offering me the top layer. 'You should eat more – the baby gets all his nourishment from you.'

I didn't dare say he got most of it from a plastic bottle. I had fed him successfully a number of times but it was very painful and the baby always seemed hungry.

'How about Billie?' Liam suggested randomly as he cradled the baby in his arms. 'He looks like a Billie, doesn't he?'

Of course he didn't. He looked like himself but I knew the name 'Billie' meant a lot to Liam. It was his mother's name. A woman he had no blood tie with yet loved with every beat of his heart. She was his adoptive mother and had died just before we met.

I nodded. What else could I do? Liam leapt up and kissed me.

'Hello, Billie Boy,' he said, picking him up and nestling him against his chest.

He looked so happy. How could I say I wanted to name the baby after you?

CHAPTER ELEVEN

The day we brought Billie home from hospital everything changed forever. I knew it would. I just had no idea how much. The roads were icy and it took us almost an hour to travel the short distance from the hospital. By the time we got home Billie was fractious but Liam insisted on ceremoniously carrying him over the threshold like some demi-god while I followed three paces behind with bags of nappies, toys and clothes.

'He doesn't need parents; he needs an entourage,' I moaned.

Liam spun round and tutted. It was the first time I'd seen him annoyed with me but it was certainly not the last.

'Welcome home little man,' he whispered as he opened the door and proudly carried his son up to the nursery; the room Liam had spent every waking moment decorating various shades of blue.

He positioned Billie in his cot. Immediately, he snuggled up to a furry pig, one of the many toys Liam had bought him, eagerly latching on, mistaking its pink snout for my nipple. As he suckled, he caught my eye, as if to say, 'The pig can do it, why can't you?' Within moments he was asleep. I left Liam watching over him and crept off to bed.

When I woke I felt elated, like a weight had been lifted. Sleep had convinced me I had wrenched the bottle of pills from you that day and you were alive and well. Ridiculously happy, I flew out of bed and into the nursery, desperate to hold you in my arms. I ran to the cot and looked in. It wasn't you. Of course, it wasn't. Shaken, betrayed by my dream, I tried to slink out of the room unnoticed but Billie opened his eyes, witnessing my exit. He began to cry.

'Is Billie okay?' Liam asked all of a panic rushing up the stairs and onto the landing. 'What's he crying for? Does he need changing?'

'What for? A puppy?' Living with him was torture, his every cry reminded me of you.

'Go back to bed and get some rest. I've got this,' Liam ordered, manoeuvring past me and disappearing inside the nursery.

I didn't like his tone. I watched from the doorway as he picked up the baby and spoke softly. At least Billie had one decent parent. From then on, I kept my distance, not because I didn't love him but because I did. You get that, don't you Mark? I loved you and look what happened.

Whenever Billie saw me he would squall, screwing up his eyes and making his face go all red.

'He's hungry,' said Liam.

'Perhaps, it's time to switch to a bottle full-time,' I suggested.

'We agreed you were going to keep feeding him, at least for the first six months.'

Six months? Six days had been more than enough.

'I can't do it. It's too painful,' I told him.

The next morning I felt awful, my breasts swollen like medicine balls, as hot as hell.

'You've got mastitis,' Doctor Pearce told me matter-of-factly, handing me a prescription for antibiotics. Any hope of a legitimate reason to stop breast-feeding was quickly dashed. 'I know it's painful but the best thing you can do is let the baby feed off both sides to reduce the pressure.'

'You are kidding?'

She shook her head and buzzed through for the next patient as she glanced at the baby lying asleep in his pram, 'If you still feel poorly in a few days, pop back and see me. Billie looks well.'

Lucky Billie.

I rushed into the waiting-room, opened my blouse and lifted the baby to my breast. He turned away.

'Latch on, please.'

His head continued to wobble unhelpfully from side to side. Obviously, he had no teeth but it still felt like a thousand incisors lacerating my inflamed nipple when he finally fed. No wonder Mum never breast-fed us. She tried with you but it didn't last long. She never did understand why feeding a baby and smoking should be mutually exclusive.

'Christ! Mark's on fire,' she would shout as she hurriedly swept the fluffy grey worms of ash off your skull. 'Don't worry, it'll make his hair grow.' Then, seeing my alarmed expression would add, 'Oi! You! Nosey Parker, don't tell yer Dad.'

Once Liam returned to work he was away from home for anything up to ten hours a day. With no one to talk to, I found myself envying other women their mothers, imagining how wonderful it must have been to have someone to fuss over them and their offspring. Don't get me wrong, Mark, I didn't want Mum. God no! She'd have changed her hairstyle more often than her grandson's nappy but it would have been nice to have had someone to guide me through.

In desperation, I went to see Doctor Pearce again. The mastitis had calmed down, which was more than could be said for me. By the time I reached the surgery, with Billie yelling all the way there in his pram, I was in a terrible state. The doctor let me talk. She listened and nodded as if she really cared. I trusted her and nearly opened up about you but managed to stop myself. It was too dangerous.

'Just to be clear,' she began and I could tell she was struggling to fully understand my ambivalence towards Billie. 'You love your baby but can't bring yourself to show him, is that right?'

Put like that it sounded so heartless. There was so much more to it than that but I couldn't tell her.

'I want to cuddle him but he doesn't like me.'

'He doesn't like you?' she repeated, unable to keep the surprise out of her voice. 'What makes you think that? What is it you're not telling me, Susan?'

Doctor Pearce was more insightful than I'd given her credit for. There was no point lying so I told her all about Mum's tablets and what had happened that day, but I was careful to leave out my part in it. When I'd finished she handed me a tissue.

'That sounds very difficult. Have you ever had any counselling?'

I shook my head. I couldn't think straight. She checked my notes, picked up her pen and added a few lines of her own.

'Y'know, it's very common to feel like this after a difficult birth. The emergency Caesarean was traumatic and you weren't able to bond with your baby immediately because he was so poorly. It wasn't your fault, Susan. Please don't blame yourself.'

I remembered one of my teachers saying the same thing after you had died: 'Don't blame yourself, Susan.' What did she know? She wasn't there.

'Do you think talking to someone might help?' asked the Doctor, reaching for her pen again.

'No,' I said quickly. 'Not that.'

The last thing I needed was some well-meaning therapist messing with my head, winkling out the truth. I'd had enough of all that after you died.

'I think you need something,' she said, writing me a prescription and handing it to me. 'Low dose anti-depressants. Just a short course to get you through this difficult patch.'

Not wanting to disobey her, particularly after she'd been so kind, I got the tablets dispensed then wondered what the hell I'd done and headed straight for the nearest public loo where I flushed them away. It was a relief to see them disappear. I couldn't risk having pills in the house with Billie, not after what had happened with you. Silly really, Billie couldn't even walk, but I had to be careful. On the way home the park and cafes were full of mums proudly showing off their babies, looking like giving birth had given them a new lease of life. How I longed to switch places and smile and laugh with my boy.

Billie refused to be bottle fed, regularly throwing up his formula milk, preferring to root around in my maternity bra, usually in front of some po-faced woman who looked like she might report me for indecent exposure. The only respite I got was when he was asleep. Then I'd have about an hour to catch up with all the chores. I hated the mess and was desperate to keep order but there was never enough time.

'God Almighty!' said Mrs Reynolds when she popped by unannounced. 'Look at the state of this place. I'll send my new girl round to give you a hand. She's very good. I'll pay. My gift. Better than another cuddly toy, eh?'

'Thanks, that would be a big help,' I told her, moving an assortment of tiny blue vests and socks off the sofa so she could sit down.

'Where is he?' she asked looking around.

'Liam's gone shopping.'

'No, not Liam, the baby. Where's Billie?'

'Sleeping.'

On cue, he let out a little cry.

'Was asleep,' corrected Mrs Reynolds. 'Come on. I wanna meet him.' Following the baby's mewling, she headed for the nursery. When I arrived, just seconds behind her, she already had him in her arms.

'Ah, hello Billie! Look at him, bless his heart. Oh, he's the image of his father, isn't he? Can't see you in him at all.'

She was right. Had Billie looked more like me perhaps I would've felt closer to him. I don't know. I doubt it was as simple as that. Mrs Reynolds stroked his head. I did that once and he cried for a full five minutes but this time, he didn't make a fuss; he even had the nerve to smile at her.

'Oh look out! He's got wind,' she said, putting him over her shoulder and rubbing his back. He obliged with a burp.

I had never seen her so happy. Unlike me, she was a natural. As far as I knew, she didn't have children. She'd never mentioned a family. Eventually, she turned her gaze away from the baby and back to me.

'You alright?'

'Fine.' I don't know why I bothered telling a lie, she was too fly for that.

'Baby not getting you down, is he? It happens. No shame in it.'

'Are you saying I can't cope?'

'No, 'cos not. You just look a bit low. A touch of the Baby Blues. It's normal, my sister had it with her first one.'

'I told you. I'm fine.'

'Well, you don't look it. Sit down, I'll make you a nice cup of tea.'

With the baby still in her arms, she disappeared into the kitchen. I followed and watched as she placed him in his seat, angling it so he could see us both. 'There Billie, you sit there and watch Mummy. There's a good boy.'

I had never seen her soft, maternal side before. I wasn't sure I liked it.

'It's time for Billie's feed, perhaps you should go.'

'I'm in no rush,' she replied, searching the cupboards.

'It's nearly time for his nap.'

'He's only just woken up,' she said, triumphantly finding the tea bags in the jar marked 'coffee'.

'Leave it,' I said, closing the fridge door she had just opened.

'What's wrong, Susan? What's wrong? I'm only trying to help. I say I'm only trying …'

'You're interfering. Just leave us alone and don't send your cleaner. I don't need her.'

She surveyed the room, littered with baby detritus and shook her head.

'You need someone. I say you need someone.'

'I don't need you coming here finding fault. I don't need you coming here finding fault,' I shouted, mimicking her habit of repeating herself when she was stressed. It was mean but I'd had enough. I was beyond reason and snatched the baby from her. He immediately started to cry.

'Oh Susan! I didn't mean to upset you, I didn't mean… oh dear… please, let me get you that tea. Sit down and relax. Sit down and … the baby knows you're a bit low. He knows you're low. They pick up on your mood. If you don't calm down you …'

I stared at her in disbelief. Mrs Reynolds was the closest person I had to a mother, which wasn't to say she was anything like a mother because she wasn't but I expected some sort of support.

'The baby's fine. Don't accuse me of …'

She turned away, bending down to kiss the baby's head.

'Bye-bye, little man, your Auntie Dot will be back to see you very soon. In the meantime, be a good boy for Mummy.'

'I'm sorry, Mrs Reynolds, I didn't mean to be rude, I'm just so tired,' I explained, going to the front door and holding it open for her.

'Apology accepted.' Her eyelids flickered, a sure sign she was fighting the urge to say it again. 'Promise me you'll have a chat to the doctor.'

'There's nothing she can do.'

'Well, at least tell Liam how you feel. He'll understand. You've got a good one there. I'll look in again soon. If you need anything, you know where I am.'

After she'd gone, I sat down and cried. Not to be outdone, Billie joined in, screaming even louder.

'You need to get Billie into a routine, that way you'd have more time for yourself,' ventured Liam when he got home. 'Regular times for his feeds and naps.'

'I know what a routine is,' I snapped, trying to secure a nappy on a wriggling baby. 'Tell him, not me.'

I threw the dirty nappy into a plastic bag, tied it tightly and chucked it on the floor. Liam quietly picked it up and put it in the bin.

'Since when did you become such an expert? You're never here. What would you know?'

He looked hurt. I had never rounded on him before, well not like that.

'Do you want to talk?' he asked, picking up the baby and cradling him in his arms. I couldn't remember the last time he had cuddled me.

'What d'you want to talk about, Liam? The sleepless nights? The dirty nappies? The endless piles of washing? Look at it! How something so small can create all this mess, God knows.'

'The baby's got a name and it's not Billie's fault. Calm down, love.' He went to put his free arm around me but I pushed him away.

'You try staying at home with him day in, day out. He won't sleep, he even refuses to drink the milk I've spent all day expressing.'

'He's no fool - breast is best,' Liam smiled.

His crass joke couldn't have been more poorly timed.

'You just clear off to work, then cruise back in, read him a story and put him to bed. You get the good bits and I get all the shit. Literally.'

I sniffed.

107

'Oh no, not again. I've only just changed him.' I picked up the baby and thrust him at Liam. Then I walked out of the house and didn't stop until a car shot past, sending a gush of cold water over my feet. It must have been raining for hours.

CHAPTER TWELVE

It's strange how things happen. You wake up to what you think is going to be just another day, then there it is, the thing you dread the most.

'Shut up! Shut up! Shut up!' Billie just kept on and on, and on, and on and on.

I could hear him as I lay in bed, desperately trying to get some sleep but kept awake by the incessant bawling that always started just after Liam left for work. Please, I thought, just five more minutes, then I'll come. But no, those five minutes were his, not mine. His yelling turned into a low, repetitive growl. He unnerved me. I was frightened of what would happen if I didn't go to him and even more terrified of what could happen if I did. The cries were the perfect pitch to snap my nerves.

'For God's sake, shut up.'

He screamed once more, then silence. I hardly dared hope he had gone back to sleep. He was bound to get a second wind and start again. I waited, straining to hear. Nothing. My body flooded with relief as I realised the sheet was wound around my right hand. Letting go, I watched as the colour returned to my knuckles. I breathed out. Thank God. The next minute he was crying again, louder this time. I started to scream. The louder he cried, the louder I roared. Wild, I got up and flew to his room, somehow just managing to stop myself at the doorway. I could see the pale blue, crocheted blanket moving in his cot, his arms and legs flailing about and all the while hear that same piercing cry. The feeling only lasted a second but I recognised it and knew I had to get away.

'What the bloody hell …?' asked Mrs Reynolds as I stood barefoot wearing just my pyjamas in her packed TV lounge.

'Out of the way,' ordered an elderly guest, grabbing my arm and shoving me aside. 'We're watching that.'

A woman pointed to the screen with her white stick. I started to laugh. What could be funnier than a blind woman watching television? No one else found it amusing, particularly not Mrs Reynolds who bundled me off into the kitchen where she lit up a cigarette in full view of her 'No smoking' sign. Even that was hysterical. I found everything, from the white paper napkins folded to resemble swans to the teapot in the shape of a thatched cottage, hilarious.

'Susan,' said Mrs Reynolds in a tone I'd never heard her use before. 'Susan.'

'Dot,' I replied, the sound of her name sending me into giggles. 'Dottie.'

She caught hold of my arms and looked me squarely in the face. I remember looking down at her thin hands and her wedding finger bejewelled with gold rings, each one encrusted with rubies and diamonds. Even in that moment, I remember thinking how strange it was that in all the time I'd been working for her, I'd never noticed them. I liked the thought that someone, most likely Mr Reynolds had, at some point, adored Mrs Reynolds. She was lovely and deserved to be loved.

110

'Susan! Whatever's going on? Where's the baby? Where's Billie?'

Hearing his name was like having a bucket of cold water thrown in my face. I stopped laughing. Nothing was funny anymore, far from it. She came close, breathing smoke in my face. She spoke with a menacing urgency.

'Susan? Is Billie okay? Where is he? Tell me. Where's Billie?'

For goodness sake, I thought, how many more times?

'He's at home.'

'Is anyone with him?'

Not again. What was wrong with her?

'He's fine, probably asleep.'

'Susan, is Liam there? Is Liam with Billie?'

The next thing I remember was sitting beside her in the back of a black cab. I couldn't think why. Surely she should have been at work? Yet there she was perched on the edge of her seat, leaning forward, giving the driver directions and shouting at him to 'bloody keep going, bloody keep going', every time he stopped at a red light. No one was more surprised than me when we pulled up outside my house. I couldn't imagine what we were doing there. I'd only just left. For the life of me, I couldn't figure out why Liam was standing at the door looking furious.

'Don't be too hard on her. Don't be hard on her,' she told him, an arm around my shoulder as she guided me inside. 'She's not well. She's not well, more to be pitied than scolded. She needs to rest. I'll put her to bed.'

'Thanks but I can look after her,' said Liam ushering her back outside.

'Mrs Reynolds, Dot, stay, please,' I protested, but neither of them took any notice.

'You can see she's not right. I say she's not right.'

'I know that,' he said, his voice level only just keeping his temper. 'She went out and left a new-born baby …'

I had no idea what he said next, his words drowned under a cascade of memories that flooded my brain like bilge. Mum applying her lipstick in the hall mirror, the flash of suspender and puckered white flesh, the tight-fitting dress and you on the stairs, fingers in your ears, not wanting her to go. No one could stop her, not even you. She left us, just like she always did. But we were older, much older than Billie yet I'd still walked away. Oh my God.

I remember Mrs Reynolds tried to manoeuvre me past Liam but he barred our way as he looked at me accusingly. What was his problem?

'Mrs Reynolds, I appreciate you ringing and bringing Susan home. If you hadn't been there I dread to think…' he paused then reached awkwardly into his pocket. 'Here, take this, for the cab fare.' He took out a note and handed it to her but she was having none of it.

'I don't want that. I don't want that. I'll look after Susan. You go and see to Billie, go and see to the baby,' she said taking charge.

Liam could see she had no intention of leaving. Reluctantly, he stepped aside as we walked past him into the hall. I can still picture his face, all twisted and taut. I gripped Mrs Reynolds' hand tightly. I could feel her rings against my fingers as she took me upstairs and tucked me into bed, fussing over the pillows, making sure the covers were just so.

'There, how's that? Comfy? You'll be fine now, Susan, you'll be fine. You just need to rest.' With that she sat on the edge of my bed and slowly stroked my forehead.

When I awoke, she'd gone. Hoping she was downstairs, I got up and put on some clothes, feeling nothing. It was as if I was a casual observer, a spectator with no say or control. It was odd. The old me, the real me, was slipping away. I couldn't let that happen. As I tiptoed downstairs I heard Liam in the kitchen, talking to Billie and fussing around as he fed him. For once the baby was silent. As quietly as I could, I let myself out of the front door and closed it softly behind me.

I don't remember how I got to the surgery. I can't tell you anything about the journey, who I saw or what the weather was like. I was just passing through, leaving no footprint.

When I arrived, the waiting room was packed. My heart sank at the sight of all those people, row upon row of anonymous faces, all listening for their names to be called. What if Doctor Pearce couldn't fit me in? I had to see her and went straight to the receptionist just as her phone rang.

'Don't answer that!' I wanted to yell but could only watch as she picked up the receiver, deftly sliding the glass partition across to shut me out.

I waited, waving my hands to get her attention but she just turned away and carried on her conversation. I tapped on the glass. She spun round and glared.

'Please,' I cried.

Covering the receiver with one hand, she pulled open the partition with the other.

'Can I help you?'

'I need to see Doctor Pearce.'

113

'I'm sorry but we're very busy. There are no walk-in appointments left.'

'It's an emergency.'

Sighing audibly, she consulted the diary. 'The earliest slot I can offer you is next Friday.'

I couldn't wait that long. I burst into tears, big juddering yelps.

'I've just had a baby and I ...'

At that moment, Doctor Pearce came out of her room.

'It's okay,' she told the receptionist. 'I'll deal with this.'

Within minutes, I was sitting in her room, clutching the very same box of tissues she'd given me the time before.

'What's the matter, Susan?' she asked gently.

It was hard to know where to begin. I cried for a long time. When I'd finished I felt a bit better, like something inside me had shifted.

'Have you given any more thought to the counselling I suggested?'

I shook my head.

'I think it would help, Susan.' Her tone was brusque, less understanding than before. I didn't like the way she looked at me yet it was impossible to tell what she was thinking. 'Are the tablets I prescribed helping?'

She knew I hadn't touched the anti-depressants. It would've been obvious from my behaviour. As I sat there watching her thread her fingers through her gold neck chain, I remembered all those tablets Mum took. Perhaps whatever was wrong with her was wrong with me too. The last thing I wanted was to turn out like her. It was a relief to be thinking a little clearer. Perhaps the gloom that had settled like mist inside my head was lifting.

'Susan,' the doctor prompted. 'Did you take the tablets?' Her tone was patronising, like she was talking to a petulant child, which, in a way, she was. Sometimes, I think I got stuck at seven years old, the same age I'd been when you died. I never grew up, not really, incapable of moving on and letting go. That's what we're all supposed to do these days, Mark. It's healthy to move on and let go. But it's not that simple. Nothing ever is.

'Susan, you need to give them time. There's no instant fix but if you stick with them, you will see a difference, I promise.'

'I don't want them.'

She sat forward in her chair, reducing the space between us. 'Generally the benefits outweigh any possible downsides.'

I shook my head. All I could see were those treacherous yellow pills dancing across the floor and settling in the shape of a map of Asia on the kitchen floor. And you, so still, your arms by your sides.

'Now listen to me, Susan. This is important. We have to think about what's best for you and your baby.'

Baby? What baby? There was no baby, just me and my little brother alone in the house.

'I can't make you see a therapist and I certainly can't force you to take the medication but you do need some support.'

I stopped listening, allowing myself to slide beneath the slipstream of her words, letting them lap over me like waves. Her voice, soft and melodious was so different from Mum's forty-fags-a-day rasp. She consulted my notes.

'How about Billie's father? You do still live with him, don't you?'

115

Billie? Who the hell was Billie? My mind was full of you, your face smiling, your hand holding the pills but why wasn't I stopping you? I had been a bystander, letting the tragedy unfold.

'I'm sure Liam would love to help …'

Ah, there it was. I kept my head very still, careful not to dislodge the picture. I could see Liam in the kitchen … a baby in his arms … our baby… Billie. Ah! Yes! I remembered. Thank God. I wasn't completely mad. I must have smiled with relief because Doctor Pearce smiled back.

'So, could he do more?'

I shook my head. Even I knew Liam did more than his fair share.

'Is there anyone else? Someone you can trust with Billie?'

Billie was my son but I wasn't his mother. Not a real one. Being a Mum was supposed to come naturally, that's what everyone tells you. Apparently, a magical maternal instinct kicks in when the baby's born. I'd barely given birth and the doctor was already saying I needed help. True, I wasn't coping. All the same, I didn't like being told to hand over my baby. God knows why I took offence, you'd have thought I'd have jumped at the chance of some respite but it smacked of giving up when I hadn't even started. You may find it hard to believe but I wanted to be a good Mum to Billie. I was just too terrified to try. It felt like I had been sitting opposite Doctor Pearce all morning. Yet there had been no examination, no treatment, no new prescription just endless questions and the suggestion of counselling. Why would I want to talk to a stranger when I've got you? I was just beginning to wonder why I'd bothered coming, when she reached over and rested her hand on my forearm.

'A break from the baby, just from time to time. How does that sound?'

It sounded like bliss. She must have seen the shadows lift from my face because she kept going, persuading me she knew best. 'Is there a relative or perhaps a friend who'd enjoy looking after Billie now and again?'

In the short time I'd known Mrs Reynolds, she had been as good as a mum to me. It followed that she would make the perfect surrogate gran for Billie. Perhaps if I'd taken her up on her offer of help in the first place things wouldn't have got so out of hand.

I couldn't wait to go home and tell Liam. He would be pleased to get back to the office full-time, instead of having to work from home. At last, things were going to get better. I was so happy I even thought I might manage an afternoon with Billie sometime. I could pack a picnic and we could go to the park, maybe ask Mrs Reynolds to join us if she wasn't too busy. Elated, I ran back through the park, this time noticing the brightly coloured flowers, and seeing the mums and their babies anew. For the first time, being part of their little gang was a real possibility. Like the doctor said, all I needed was a little help.

CHAPTER THIRTEEN

'Me? Help you look after the baby? You mad? I've only just got over the menopause.'

I watched Mrs Reynolds stack four triangular pieces of white toast into a stainless steel rack as she prepared breakfast for her one weekend guest that morning.

'But you said if there was anything you could do to …' I began, feeling panicky before automatically falling into my old waitressing role and fetching a tray.

'I never said nothing of a sort. I've got this place to run. I can't be running off every five minutes because Billie wants changing. Here, where you going with that? Give it a wipe over first.' She handed me the dishcloth and I cleaned the non-existent stain off the tray, anything to hurry things along. 'Where's the strawberry jam?' she muttered, picking through a box of assorted preserves.

'Mrs Reynolds,' I said, unable to hide my desperation. 'Dot, please.'

She smiled, just for a moment, and I noticed her orange lipstick. Enthusiastically applied, the colour was too garish against her sallow complexion. I imagined it was the colour she had worn and stuck with for over forty years. Again, just for a moment, I considered telling her about you, Mark.

'I need you,' I told her.

'You don't need me. You need yer Mum.'

I bridled. I'd never mentioned Mum to her. At least I didn't think I had. Why would I? Mark, I know you loved her and she loved you in her own way but she was someone who should never have had children. I prayed I wasn't like her.

'I haven't got a ...' I faltered.

She raised her eyebrows at me. I didn't want to lie, not to her.

'Well, I have but not a real one.'

'You only get one Mum, Susan. You only get one Mum.'

She was right, I felt bad about denying Mum, even though she'd been so awful. God, Mark, you'd still be here if it wasn't for her and her stupid bloody pills. But I can't blame her. I can't blame her for everything, can I?

'I haven't seen her for years,' I explained. 'It's complicated.'

'What's complicated about picking up the phone and talking to your own mother? I'm sure she'd be over the moon to know she's got such a beautiful grandson.' Turning away from me, she flicked on the kettle, meaning I had to shout over the noise.

'We don't get on. Never have. Never will,' I said, taking the milk out of the fridge and pouring some into a jug.

She spun round, her eyes like flint. 'That's very harsh, Susan. Very harsh. Don't talk like that, I say don't talk like that about your mum. She brought you into this world.'

'But you don't know her. Don't know what she's like. What she's capable of. I'm not letting her anywhere near Billie.' As I heard myself say those words, I remember being strangely pleased with myself, strong even. At long last, I knew what it felt like to be protective towards my son.

120

'You won't let your Mum look after Billie but you'd let me?'

'You're like a mum to me.'

Her face lit up, her expression a mixture of shock and delight.

'Next you'll be saying I'm Billie's nan.' She sniffed but her grin told me she rather liked the idea.

'So you'll do it?'

'I'm not promising anything,' she said, pouring the boiling water into a stainless steel pot and throwing in a tea bag. She let the lid clatter shut. 'I might be able to spare an hour or so after I've done the breakfasts.'

I ran over and kissed her powdery cheek. It felt odd. I'd never kissed anyone apart from Liam. Not even you. I remember Mrs Reynolds smelt of tobacco and sandalwood soap.

'Enough of that. I'm going to have to completely redo the rota. Never mind, my new girl will be glad of the extra hours.' She gave me a wink, then went to the foot of the stairs and shouted up. 'Just popping out for a bit. Come down and hold the fort, there's a good girl.' She put on her coat and took her purse from the drawer where she kept it hidden under a pile of raffia placemats. 'Come on, Susan. We're going shopping. Bet you don't even know what nappies to buy, do you?'

She was right. I left all that to Liam. I had no idea what Billie needed so she took me to the supermarket and showed me.

'Put them back,' she'd say when I went for the big brands instead of the own labels. 'These are the same but cheaper.' She piled the trolley full. Even though she had hunted down the bargains, the bill still came to over a hundred pounds. I reached for my credit card. 'Put it away,' she told me, unzipping her wallet and pushing a wad of notes into the cashier's hand.

I packed the bags, it was the least I could do and carried them to the bus stop. When we got home, Liam opened the door, the baby in his arms. When Billie saw me he started to cry. We were back to square one. My heart sank. At least you were always pleased to see me.

'Let's have a hold,' Mrs Reynolds said, taking him from Liam. 'Handsome little chap! He's got your eyes, hasn't he?'

Liam said nothing but was clearly flattered, seeing Billie not as a person in his own right but as an extension of himself. Unlike me, he had well and truly bonded with his son.

'Mrs Reynolds is going to help out,' I said, thinking he'd be pleased I was taking an interest and wanted to learn how to be a better mum. For some reason I couldn't fathom at the time, he plucked the baby from her. If I'd known then what I know now I would have handled the situation very differently. 'She's going to come every day and help out.'

'I'm going to do no such thing,' said Mrs Reynolds sharply. 'No such thing. Whatever gave you that idea? I've just popped round to say hello to Billie.'

'Perhaps you should leave, this isn't a good time.' Liam's voice was hard. He was usually so reasonable, so polite.

'Liam, please! She's only trying to help,' I said, wondering what the hell had got into him. 'I'm sorry, Mrs Reynolds. Please stay. It's okay.'

She made a point of glancing around the kitchen littered with feeding bottles, drums of formula, stained bibs and an ever-increasing pile of my old newspapers stacked by the back door. When I should have been looking after Billie, I hide behind the pages of a paper or a book, lost in someone else's story.

'Looking after a baby single-handedly is hard work,' Liam told her defensively. I knew the barbed comment was meant for me but Mrs Reynolds lobbed it back.

'Oh, Liam, I bet you can't wait to get back to the office for a rest! I say, I bet you can't wait to get back to work.'

I didn't get it. The last thing I wanted was Liam in the office all day, leaving me alone with Billie. Even if Mrs Reynolds did help out, it wouldn't be full-time and I wasn't ready to be left alone with a baby. Even I knew that. It was touch and go whether I should be let anywhere near him.

'Liam loves spending time with his boy,' I told her.

'Of course he does but he needs a break. Look, the poor man's done in.'

Whatever she was trying to do Liam wasn't falling for it. 'Caring for a newborn baby is very tiring. It might be a bit much for you, at your age.'

I gasped but she seemed determined not to take the bait. 'Standing here bandying insults won't help Billie.'

Dear Mrs Reynolds, older and so much wiser than me, was not fazed. It was me she had come to help, not him. She glanced at Billie who, as if responding to a secret signal, threw up over Liam. She took the baby and handed Liam a tea-towel. He snatched it from her and used it to rub vigorously at his jumper, only succeeding in spreading the mess.

'I can pop round tomorrow morning, once I've finished the breakfasts, if it would help,' she suggested with a sly smirk. 'Your boss must want you back in the office. All this working from home's fine for a while but you must be worried someone's going to jump into your shoes.'

123

I knew by the way he kept an eye on the trade press that Liam was missing the buzz of the office. Nevertheless, for some reason, he baulked at the idea of Mrs Reynolds stepping into the breach. 'I'm sure you've got enough to do with the B&B.'

'On the contrary, it would be my pleasure to look after Billie for a bit,' she said, gently stroking his head.

'Thank you,' I said before Liam could dissuade her.

Having her around would be a golden opportunity to discover if I dared be around Billie. I couldn't let the chance to be a better mum slip away.

'How soon can you start?' I asked.

'Tomorrow? Mid-morning?'

'Hang on,' cut in Liam. 'You can't just turn up and expect to be left in charge of my son. Do you have any qualifications? Any children of your own even?' He made to take the baby from her but even he could see Billie was content, nestled in the crook of her arm.

Refusing to meet Liam's gaze, she was clearly upset. 'What a question? I say what a question? I've done...'

Nothing made any sense to me at that time and I just remember being even more confused by Liam's attitude. I thought he'd jump at the chance of someone to hold my hand and show me how to cope.

'Mrs Reynolds looked after me when I had no one; she can certainly take care of Billie. Please, let's just give it a go.'

'This is Billie we're talking about. He's my son. I'm not leaving him with just anybody.'

'But she's not just anybody. She's Mrs Reynolds.'

He scoffed. I smiled unconvincingly at her. I had to get him to agree. If anyone could bring out the mum in me, she could. Just being around her helped. A few well-chosen words from her made the torment in my head stop long enough to get some peace.

'Let's give it a go,' I said, desperate to persuade him. 'You can go for a run or focus on your work. It must be impossible to concentrate with Billie crying. You can get back to what you love doing, your job.'

He opened his mouth and I knew what he really wanted to say was that I was a terrible mother who never so much as cuddled Billie and if I would just do my fair share there would be no need for Mrs Reynolds or anyone else to step in but he didn't say that. He just pulled his pinched face and told her, 'She's not well, she needs me here.'

'Susan,' said Mrs Reynolds, making a point of emphasising my name. 'Susan is fine. She just needs a hand getting through these first few months.'

Even I didn't believe her; I'd run out on Billie once, who was to say I wouldn't do it again? Meanwhile, oblivious to the mayhem around him, the baby had fallen asleep in her arms. She certainly got his vote. I could've, should've kissed him but of course, I couldn't, didn't. What the hell was wrong with me? Liam was right; I was a poor excuse for a mother. Meanwhile, Mrs Reynolds was doing exactly the right thing, tending to the baby.

'You're a good boy, aren't you?' she murmured placing him in his Moses basket. 'No trouble. No trouble at all.'

Liam watched her every move. 'Okay,' he muttered reluctantly, as he left the room. 'Come tomorrow but just for an hour. I'll be here, working. Let's see how you get on.'

Mrs Reynolds winked at me. I smiled, relieved. Thanks to her, Liam had finally changed his tune. Back then, his

125

attitude made no sense. Perhaps if I hadn't been in such a state I would've seen what was staring me in the face. I learnt a lot from Mrs Reynolds that day but not nearly so much as I was to discover.

CHAPTER FOURTEEN

That first morning went well. Mrs Reynolds turned up, on time, ready for work. Nothing fazed her, not even when Liam kept popping into the kitchen on some spurious excuse. 'Everything okay?' he would ask as he made himself yet another coffee. Adults can be very odd, Mark, very sly and deceitful.

'Baby's asleep. Don't disturb him,' she told him crisply as he hunted in the drawer for what I suspected was a non-existent phone number on a non-existent pad. 'But now you're here, Susan and me could kill a cup of tea.'

He gave her an odd look. 'Sorry, I'm busy.'

'Don't let me keep you,' she said sarcastically as he hurried back upstairs.

She winked at me and put the kettle on. Like I said, Mark, she was a smart lady. With her by my side, I was more than happy to spend time with Billie. He didn't cry nearly so much and when he did she explained why. 'He wants feeding,' 'He needs changing,' 'He wants a nap.'

Knowing what was wrong was one thing, having the confidence to do something about it, quite another. Of course, I knew how to give a baby a bottle, change its nappy and rock it to sleep; I'd spent years looking after you. That was the problem. As soon as Billie needed something doing, I froze, a response Mrs Reynolds had no truck with. The first couple of times, she showed me what to do then more or less did it for me but when I asked her a third time she bridled. 'Can't you see I'm busy, Susan?'

'Busy' usually meant lighting up another cigarette. She puffed away in the garden, her back towards the window, looking away from the house. 'Have you changed that baby yet?' she called over her shoulder as she dropped the butt onto the path and ground it with the heel of her shoe. I watched in horror as she opened a fresh packet and pulled out another cigarette using her teeth.

'I can't do it,' I protested, my palms sweating.

'Yes, you can.'

Tending to Billie was nothing like looking after you. For a start you were older when Mum first left me alone with you. It was just after your third birthday. She gave you a teddy. I remember it had orange fur and a blue ribbon tied in a bow around its neck. She sat the three of us around the kitchen table, put some custard creams on a plate and told you it was a teddy bears' picnic. While you were busy feeding the bear biscuits, she told me she was nipping out for some lemonade. It was dark by the time she got home. At least, you could talk and try and tell me what you wanted. With Billie, it was guesswork. The only good thing was he stayed in one spot. Mum said she needed 'eyes in the back of her head' with you. Most of the time she was right but that afternoon, I saw what you were doing all too clearly.

'Ain't you done it yet? Poor Billie, give him here.' Mrs Reynolds was indoors, standing next to me, coughing into her hand while still clutching her cigarettes and lighter. Without a word she deftly set about changing his nappy. When she'd finished she settled him back in his cot, then turned to me. 'So, what's this all about?'

I didn't want to tell her but the words stuck for so long in my head were desperate to be heard. 'Mrs Reynolds, I killed my brother. I killed Mark.'

Her head swivelled like an owl's towards me. 'Do what? I say, do what?'

And then I told her. I told her everything. Well, my version but even that had changed so much over the years I didn't know what was true and what I'd made up to make myself sound less of a monster. When I'd finished, she didn't speak, just stared at me, her face crumpled, looking like she might burst into tears. She glanced at the phone on the wall and for one awful minute I thought she was going to call the police but she just got up and put her arms around me. She held me for a long time even though I didn't deserve kindness. 'You poor girl. You poor, poor girl.'

'Mrs Reynolds, I don't think you understand...'

'Oh I do, Susan. I understand more than you'll ever know, believe me. Now, you've got to put that all behind you. You didn't kill him. You couldn't kill no one. It weren't your fault, obviously a tragic accident.'

I wanted to believe her. Of course I did but I knew differently. I was there.

'But I ...'

'Stop blaming yourself. What's done is done. Billie's the important one now.'

'But I'm no good for him'

'You listen to me. You're his mother. You're not goin' to harm Billie. Anyone can see you love the bones of him.'

129

Then she picked him up and gave him to me before going outside for another cigarette. Neither of us ever spoke about it again. There was no need. I'd told her what had happened and she'd told me what she thought had happened. 'Leave it now,' she'd say if I looked like I was going to start.

I wish you could've met her, Mark. You'd have liked her. And she'd have loved you. Imagine how different things would have been if we'd had her for a mum. You'd still be here. She had a way with her, a way of convincing me I wasn't the useless mother I thought I was. Thanks to her, I had a new, more forgiving mantra. If I said it enough times, I might start to believe it.

'You can do it, Susan. You can do it.' See, I even repeated myself just like she did.

After a while I became a dab hand at looking after Billie and loved the warm feeling of him in my arms as I fed him his bottle. I enjoyed the ritual of making up the formula milk and hearing him sigh with satisfaction when he downed the last drop before giving me a look as if to say, 'You're getting there.'

True, things didn't always go according to plan. Trust me, nothing ever does. Billie often used to wait until she was out of sight then make that awful piercing noise he saved just for me. Any decent mother would have been by his side in a heartbeat. Not me. 'Mrs Reynolds! Billie's crying.'

'I can hear that.'

'He wants you,' I would tell her as I backed away from the baby as if he was a wasp.

'He wants YOU, Susan.'

The crying would get louder and louder until it reached that God-awful pitch that messed with my head.

'Make him stop.'

'You make him stop. Hurry up. The screaming's bringing on one of me heads.'

It was the hugging, the holding that got me. What if I picked him up and squeezed him just a bit too tight? I remember one time, peering into his Moses basket and shaking, really trembling. All the while Billie was making this funny whimpering sound. Mrs Reynolds was in the toilet. I could hear her humming which usually meant she was going to be some time. There was nothing else for it. Carefully, I slid my hands around him, feeling his soft warm flesh against my hands. Far from straining and pushing away like he usually did, he snuggled in, still grizzling. I'm ashamed to say my instinct was not to soothe him as it should have been, but to put him in his cot and run. To this day I don't know what made me change my mind but for the first time ever I held onto him, giving him my little finger to suck just like I'd seen Liam do countless times. Gradually the whimpering subsided and I heard myself say, 'Mummy loves you.'

I can still hear Mum saying those words to you as I stood listening, behind the door, out of sight. I'm sure she knew I was there but she didn't care, never feeling the need to repeat the words to me. My insides would twist and my tummy would go all bubbly. The feeling went after a while but it was horrible while it lasted. I didn't want Billie to ever feel that way. 'Mummy loves you,' I repeated.

I liked the sound of the words. After I had given up all hope, it had finally happened. I loved my baby, and it was all thanks to Mrs Reynolds. I'm not sure how long she had been standing there but when I finally took my eyes off Billie, there she was smiling at the pair of us.

'That toilet won't flush. Liam will have to have a look at it. Oh my God, is that the time?' she asked looking at her watch. 'So much for only staying an hour.'

As time went on, she was still reluctant to hand me the reins. It was odd, one minute forcing responsibility on me, the next not trusting me. I wish I'd never trusted her and told her my secret. What a fool I'd been. I half expected the police to turn up and arrest me. After a while, I realised I was being silly. The only reason she came round was because she enjoyed the company. I certainly looked forward to her visits. For one thing, it was an incentive to get dressed, no more slopping around in my dressing gown, hair unwashed, legs unshaved. Instead I'd shower and put on fresh clothes before brushing my hair. It was just the usual stuff normal people take for granted but you have to remember Mark, back then I wasn't normal. Far from it.

Feeling better than I had for ages, I'd race downstairs every morning to be greeted by Billie in his Dad's arms, waving at me. It was like a wonderful new beginning every day. 'Hello, my beautiful boy,' I'd say, hugging him to me.

Even then, when everything was just getting good, Liam couldn't resist giving me his pinched face, the one that said he didn't entirely trust me with his son, always ensuring there was no gap between him leaving and Mrs Reynolds arriving.

'Ain't you gone yet? You can't be late for work, ' she'd say, taking off her coat and hanging it over the banister. 'Ain't you gone yet?'

Although he still didn't seem to like her, after a while, he was more than happy to let her care for Billie. Back then, I couldn't understand his change of heart but as time went on, it became obvious.

Despite her confidence in me, there was still something not quite right. I couldn't put my finger on it but whatever it was made me glad the handovers between Liam and Mrs Reynolds left no margin for error. You see Mark, I knew me loving Billie was no guarantee of anything. I loved you.

Then one day, just as the routine was really working, Mrs Reynolds kicked away the crutch. 'The B&B's very busy. I'm fully booked for the foreseeable.'

We both knew it was a lie. The B&B was not so much a destination of choice for the people who washed up on her doorstep, as a last resort. Even being classified as a B&B was pushing it. The beds were uncomfortable and the breakfasts inedible. The only thing it had going for it was the room rate. Like most of the furnishings it had remained the same for over twenty years.

'Please stay,' I said unable to bear the thought of going back to the way things were with Liam shadowing my every move. 'I can pay you.'

She shot me a look and immediately it was clear I'd hurt her feelings. 'You think I'm doing this for the money? Money?'

'Sorry, Dot.'

She took a breath and exhaled, visibly softening. 'I'll stay 'til the end of the week. You will be fine, Susan. And don't worry about His Lordship. I'll soon have him back at work full-time and out of your hair.'

If there was one thing worse than having Liam at home, it was not having Liam at home. I loved Billie, I really did, even more than you but I still lacked confidence. 'Can't we leave things as they are, just for a bit?'

'I've got a business to run. Them eggs aren't goin' fry themselves.'

'But you do the breakfasts before you come.'

'Excuse me?' she fixed me with glare. 'I'm not your glorified nanny. You, young lady, have gotta get on with it. I haven't got time to keep coming round here. You won't be the first woman what thinks they can't cope and you won't be the last.'

I could see straight through her. Even so, her cruel-to-be-kind tactics still hurt. 'Billie will miss you.'

'You mean you'll miss me. When I think of the state this place was in when I showed up. Good job I turned up when I did. I say it's a good job I turned up when I did.'

I went to hug her.

'Hug Billie, not me. Go on, give him a cuddle.' She left the room and I heard her soft tread on the stairs. When she came back a few moments later I could tell by her eyes she'd been crying. 'Right, then. That's that, one more week, I say one more week. After that you're on your own; except you won't be.'

I didn't catch on at first and shook my head, not understanding.

'Who else will help me?'

'Billie. When he wants something, he'll soon tell you. Don't worry, you'll both be fine.'

A few days later, I went downstairs to discover Liam pressing a white shirt, being very particular about the collar and cuffs, guiding the nose of the iron carefully across the fabric.

'What are you doing?' I asked stupidly.

'I'm going back to work today. Mrs Reynolds is right, it's career suicide for me to be out of the loop for too long.'

I knew Mrs Reynolds meant well but I still didn't feel I could cope on my own. 'But I need you here, Liam.'

'No, you don't. You just needed time. Come here.' He hugged me to him. It felt odd after so long. 'I'm sorry, Susan.' His apology took me by surprise. It was genuine, sincere. I remembered the tone from long before Billie was born. That's another thing you need to know, Mark, people change all the time. You never know quite where you are. Life is one big guessing game with no prizes. 'I mean it, I'm sorry.'

'Don't apologise. I was a mess.'

He went to kiss me but I turned away, presenting him with my cheek.

'It's going to be okay. Mrs Reynolds knows you can cope and so do I.'

Good old Mrs Reynolds, there it was again, that wonderful word. 'Can'. I took Liam's face in my hands and kissed his mouth, sinking into him, just like I did in those first heady weeks together, before any of this. It felt good. Liam was right. Everything was going to be okay. It was funny but it was as if Billie sensed the love between us. Perhaps it was just wishful thinking on my part but he looked happier. I ran over and stroked his peachy cheek with my forefinger. He smiled, I'm sure he did. When Liam finally left for work, he kissed Billie goodbye and the baby made a grab for his hair. Liam indulged him for a few moments, letting him rub his sticky palm over his hair, making it all matted.

'Okay, little man. Daddy's gotta go. Be a good boy for Mummy.'

Those words filled me with joy. I still didn't feel worthy of the title but I was going to try and live up to it. With my boy lodged contentedly in my arms, I stood at the door and waved Liam off until he reached the end of the road when he turned left and disappeared from view. Despite what Mrs Reynolds had said, I knew she wouldn't be able to keep away and by mid-morning I made sure Billie and I were ready and waiting, kettle on.

CHAPTER FIFTEEN

One of the guests discovered Mrs Reynolds collapsed in the dining room. Whoever it was had gone back in after breakfast to look for his reading glasses and there she was on the floor, one shoe on, one shoe off. My first thought was she must've looked like you did, face down, not moving. She was lucky, being found so quickly.

When Liam told me she'd had a stroke, I crumpled, coiled into a ball, like a dog making itself as small as possible, hoping not to be noticed, hoping not to be kicked.

'What's the matter with you?' asked Liam. 'It's not like she was your mum or anything.' His voice, sliced through my soft flesh, cutting my nerves. How could he be so cruel? He knew what she meant to me. He knew the difference she had made. 'She's like a mum to me.'

He replied with a snort. At the time, his callous attitude made no sense. If only he had been honest and told me what he knew, things might have been different. I still don't know why he kept quiet. That's the thing, Mark. It's hard enough working out what's going on in your own head, let alone anyone else's.

One thing I knew for certain was Mrs Reynolds didn't deserve to suffer, struck down like that, on her swirly-patterned, beer-stained carpet. I hated to think of her, alone, frightened, not having a clue what was happening. I blamed myself, certain I'd missed some clue that she wasn't well when she'd been with me the day before. Perhaps I'd asked too much, expecting her to help out with Billie as well as run the B&B but she'd never seemed stressed, just the opposite, always so capable and unflappable. There was obviously more going on beneath that calm veneer than I realised. I did my best to explain how I felt to Liam, but he wasn't interested, not really. I could tell by the way he rubbed his ear that his mind was elsewhere. Yet, just occasionally, he could find the right words. That's the remarkable thing about people, they surprise you and that's what keeps you hanging in there, Mark. Hope.

'Liam, she was always there for me but where was I when she needed someone?

'Exactly where you should've been, exactly where she wanted you to be, with Billie.'

When I heard those kind words, he became the man I'd fallen in love with again. It was all too much.

'Hey, come on! Don't cry, Susan. She wouldn't want you to be upset. I say, she wouldn't want you to be upset,' he repeated, just like she would have done. That one, badly-timed joke at Mrs Reynolds' expense changed my mood in an instant. I don't expect you to understand, Mark, but it's often what people do when something bad happens. They deal with it by trying to be funny. The one time it didn't happen was with you. Nobody laughed then. Looking back I think losing you broke Mum. True, she was always on the edge but it tipped her over. Dad dealt with it differently. He shut down and shut me out.

The next thing I knew, Liam was frowning and I was giggling. Don't ask me why. I didn't want to but I was laughing through my tears. The two opposing emotions collided, knocking me off balance. In an instant, my smile evaporated and I began to cry again, setting Billie off. Instead of going to him like Mrs Reynolds would've wanted me to, I ran out of the room. I knew it was wrong but it was all I could do. I threw myself on the stairs howling like an animal. Liam came after me and gave me that look, the one that said he still didn't trust me with Billie. I didn't blame him but I never forgave him either.

Unfortunately, Mrs Reynolds' stroke was more serious than I had imagined. When I saw her a few days later, she was nothing like the woman I remembered and was completely thrown when her sister let me into the B&B. She looked just like Dot but had a strong Scottish accent.

'Come on in, Susan. Pleased to meet you. I'm Deirdre. Thanks for phoning and popping round. She's in the back room.'

I followed her through. The place already smelt different, all pine air-freshener and disinfectant. As soon as Mrs Reynolds saw me she rose up in her chair before collapsing back down.

'Hello, Dot.'

She made a noise.

'She's got aphasia,' Deirdre explained in her heavy Scottish brogue, emphasising the word as if I was deaf. 'She understands you but can't think of the right words to say back. The doctor says you can still talk to her though.'

'How are you, Dot?' What an inane question. I could've kicked myself but she wasn't bothered, too intent on staring at me like she was trying to figure out who I was.

'Billie really misses you,' I said. 'Liam too.' We say the stupidest things when we're stressed, Mark. I think we feel we have to say something even if it is inane. Her face set into a grimace.

'She gets confused, don't you, Dot? Would you like a cup of tea, Susan?

I nodded, grateful to have some time alone with Mrs Reynolds. I reached for her hand and gave it a little squeeze. She tried to smile at me. I was still babbling on about Billie, not knowing what else to say when Deidre came in with the drinks.

'She doesn't have a clue who you are. Sugar?'

I shook my head, amazed at the way this woman could distance herself from her sister's plight. I looked away as I fought back the tears.

'I've got a florists in Edinburgh. I've had to shut up shop. I can't stay here forever but I'm all she's got. I say, I'm all she's got.'

The repetition took me by surprise. Obviously a family trait, shame she wasn't more like her sister in other ways. I didn't like Deirdre. Dot had never mentioned her so I can't imagine they were close. Families can be like that, Mark, you share the same blood but not the same heart.

'God knows when she's going be right. I say God knows. The doctors won't commit themselves. I don't think they know. Every case is different. One of my customers had three strokes and was as right as rain. Look at her. Like a vegetable, so she is.'

Without drinking my tea, I kissed Dot goodbye.

When I got home, I went straight to bed, grateful for the duvet to pull over my head and shut out the world. Apart from visits to the bathroom, I lay there for days, listening to the seemingly incessant whirr of the washing machine competing with the rising swell of Billie's crying. I guess he must have missed her. She had knitted herself into the fabric of his day, as much a part of his life as she was mine. He needed to hear her voice, to know she was there, just like I did.

'He wants you,' said Liam appearing in the bedroom doorway with Billie in his arms, a red-faced bundle of furious fists and feet, lashing out.

I turned away.

'At least get up and give him a hug.'

I lay there, saying nothing, studying the wallpaper, small sprigs of yellow roses each tied with a pink bow.

'For God's sake, he needs you.'

The ribbon was too big for the stem.

'Susan, I thought we were over this. I thought you were better. Mrs Reynolds isn't here so I need you to do your bit.'

Each bud was tight, destined never to open, never to flower and flourish.

'Susan! Take him.'

'I can't.'

'Don't you mean, 'won't'?'

The pig.

'I hate you so much, Liam, I could kill you.'

'Yes, right now, I think you're capable of anything.'

Then, he just walked away, with Billie balanced on his hip, like a permanent appendage.

'You bastard.' I should never have said it. Calling an adopted person a bastard was unforgivable. Even I knew that, but Liam didn't react. I suppose it was the least of his worries.

It wasn't long before he took to sleeping in the spare room. I wasn't surprised. The sad thing was I didn't care. He'd changed and become so pompous, so self-righteous. This must be hard for you to understand, Mark. How could I be madly in love with him one minute yet mad with him the next? Apart from you, Liam was the only person who had ever loved me but I'd managed to push him a million miles away and there wasn't a thing I could do about it.

We went for days without speaking. It wasn't like when we were little, forever falling out and making up again. Sadly, most adults don't have that ability. We bear grudges, play games, score points.

Days yawned into nights as I lay in bed talking to you, still trying to make sense of that afternoon, going over every detail. If I could come to terms with what had happened, find some answers, then maybe, just maybe, I could make things right for Billie.

'Who are you chatting to?' asked Liam, passing by my bedroom door.

'No one.'

'I heard you. You sounded upset.' Just for a moment, his voice softened and there was my lovely Liam again. I wanted to tell him but I couldn't say, 'I was talking to my dead brother, Mark. I killed him, that's why I can't be with our baby.'

Liam got upset when I didn't answer. 'Have you taken your tablets, today?' he asked, suspiciously casting around for the bottle of pills he had recently collected from the chemist. 'You haven't, have you? For God's sake, we can't carry on like this. It's not fair on Billie. Or me.'

I stared at him, empty, drained of emotion, the words all used up.

'This shit ends here, Susan. I've given up hope of you being a wife but you've got to start being a Mum.'

I wasn't listening. I was still hoping to make sense of it all.

'I've lost my bloody job, thanks to you.' He was standing there, shaking with rage, waiting for me to respond. He was right, I was to blame. I was the problem. 'Did you hear me? I said I've lost my job! Well, say something, you selfish ...'

'You have no idea what you're talking about. If I was selfish, I'd do what I wanted and I'd be with Billie every minute of every day but this isn't about me.'

'What d'you mean?'

How could I tell him the stuff about Mum and Dad, about you and everything that happened that day? Looking back perhaps I should've done, perhaps he'd have understood. Who knows? There's a saying, Mark, 'Walk a mile in my shoes.' It means don't judge before you've been through the same thing because it's only then you know what it's really like. But Liam was in no mood for me.

'I can't do this anymore, Susan. I've had enough. Do you understand? Either you sort yourself out or I'm leaving. And I'm taking Billie with me.'

My stomach was empty, I hadn't eaten in days, but I still managed to be sick in the bathroom sink, holding onto both taps for support as I turned them on full blast to wash away the bile. If I hadn't been so wrapped up in the past, I'd have seen Liam had had enough. It was the wake-up call I needed. In that moment, I knew what I had to do. Talking to you hadn't helped and Mrs Reynolds was no longer around for support. The time had come to shine a light into the shadows cast by the past. I hadn't seen Mum for over ten years and she was off her face then.

CHAPTER SIXTEEN

The last I'd seen of saw of Mum was her right eye peering at me through the ever-decreasing gap in the wardrobe door as she locked me in that afternoon. Finding her would be easy. All I had to do was track down Porky Rawlings. It didn't take long. I just followed my nose and sure enough, there he was, years older, a good three stone fatter, propping up the bar in a washed-up pub just around the corner from where we used to live. Believe it or not, I recognised him straightaway. He even had the same hair-style, there was just less of it, unlike his beer belly which had ballooned to pregnancy proportions. I had guessed Mum would still be with him. After all, she'd left her husband and daughter for him. More importantly, she needed a man. Not that Porky fitted that description.

I stood by the flashing fruit machines, watching him, trying to figure out how this red, bloated man had stolen Mum away from us, but it's easy to grab what's there for the taking, Mark. All the same I couldn't help thinking how different our lives might have been had it not been for him. You'd still be here. It must've been him she'd gone to meet that afternoon. That's the worst part. I lost you because she found him. Sorry, Mark, you don't want to hear all this. There's no point in trying to shift the blame. Porky wasn't there. I was. It was my fault. Time I faced up to it.

Before approaching Porky I caught the barman's eye and ordered a vodka and orange. Dutch courage. That's what we call it when we don't have the guts to do something without a drink inside us, Mark. The barman set the glass down in front of me.

'Have one yourself,' I told him as I handed over a note. I needed a favour. I had to check with him I'd got the right bloke, just in case. 'That man, over there, at the end of the bar...'

'Porky, y'mean?'

My mouth was dry, my palms wet. I took a slug of my drink. What the hell was I doing? I shrank back behind a pillar, hoping to slink out of the pub unnoticed. Just then Porky turned around and drained his glass, giving me the perfect opening line.

'Can I get you another?' I asked, stepping into view. Judging by his appearance, I can't imagine he was used to women throwing themselves at him but nonetheless he accepted immediately.

'Very kind of you, love,' he replied, holding out his sticky pint glass to the barman. 'Best offer I've had all day. Here, Kev, stick another in there, mate.'

Fumbling for my purse, I knocked over my drink, smashing the glass, the liquid pooling across the vinyl floor. I bobbed down to pick up the pieces.

'Leave it, you'll cut yerself,' said Porky, sucking the foam from the top if his pint with thin purple lips. 'Ere, Kev, got a dustpan and brush?'

Slowly, I stood up. He squinted at me over the top of his glass as he continued to sup.

'Ave we met?' Coming from anyone else it may have sounded like a chat-up line but not from Porky.

'I'm Susan.'

I waited, searching his face for some sort of further recognition. What was I expecting? The last time he'd seen me I was a little girl; I can't imagine the meeting had even registered on his radar. All I'd been was some other bloke's kid. There was no point playing games.

'I think you know my mum.' The word 'know' was something of an understatement unless I had been using it in the biblical sense, a reference sure to be lost on Porky, and you, Mark. You don't need to know what it means but it's all about getting close to someone, very close. 'You're Porky, aren't you?'

I suppressed a grin as it struck me how his nickname, once an ironic joke, now fitted him perfectly. He had grown into it. Literally. On hearing his name, he sprung forward, put down his glass and licked his lips, his eyes fixed on me.

'Who are you?'

'I told you. Susan.'

'Susan? But she was only so big.' He held out his hand to waist height, alternately lowering and lifting it by four or five inches. 'God! You've grown.'

'It's been a long time.'

'What, ten, twelve years?'

'Longer.'

I fiddled with the clasp on my purse and took out the few remaining coins, just enough money to refill his glass and loosen his tongue. Drink's good at that, Mark. It's amazing what people will say when they've had a few. I needed him to tell me where Mum was. The barman pulled another pint and lined it up on the bar. Porky thanked me by addressing his next remark to my chest. 'Yeah, you certainly have grown.'

I pulled my cardigan around me, flattening my chest as he continued to leer. 'I'm looking for Mum. D'you know where she is?'

'Ain't seen her in years,' he replied quickly, unaware I'd just seen her coming out of the toilet, her grey head bowed. Unaware I was watching her, she stopped to light her cigarette, asking a young man sitting at one of the tables to borrow his matches. He struck one and I could hear her laughing in that odd way of hers. I remember thinking, 'Go on, you enjoy yourself because you'll have nothing to smile about in a minute.' My stomach churned as I waited for her to look up. When our eyes finally met I expected at least a flicker of recognition, but nothing, Mark.

Just as I was about to step forward and talk to her, Porky shouted something I couldn't make out. She paid no attention, just continued to thank the young man for the light. Eventually, she gave up trying to flirt with him and staggered towards the bar. She was much thinner than I remembered. She stood, swaying slightly, her heavily made-up eyes unable to focus. What was I expecting, to get together with her over tea, all gingham tablecloths and pretty china? And, us leaving the past behind, recounting only the good bits and reshaping the bad into something more palatable over slices of Victoria Sponge? Let me tell you, Mark, life rarely turns out how you expect.

'Oi! You slag! He's my husband,' Mum slurred, rushing at me. 'Keep your hands off him!'

Porky, although clearly flattered she thought a young woman might be interested in him, was quick to set her right. 'Silly cow, she ain't my fancy woman. I'd pick a better-looking one than that.'

I shot him a glance.

'I'm Susan,' I said. I could have helped her out by calling her 'Mum' but I hadn't thought of her in that way for a long time.

'She ain't nothing to do with me,' said Porky. Mum gave him an odd look like she didn't understand or believe what he was saying.

'It's yer daughter, for Chrissake.'

A look, nothing like love, moved like a cloud across her face. Then I noticed something else behind her eyes, fear maybe? Me turning up out of the blue must've freaked her out, but even so, I couldn't bring myself to quell her anxiety. No one said anything for a long time. The only sound was Porky gulping his drink.

'That's not her,' said Mum, pointing her finger at me. I noted the chipped, red nail polish brushed over bitten nails. She really had let herself go.

Porky looked at his empty glass, then at my purse, then back at his glass. When another top-up was not forthcoming he snapped, 'Say what you've come to say and clear off.'

'I need to talk to her but not here.'

He shrugged.

'You've aged,' said Mum, suddenly staring at me.

'So have you,' I muttered, knowing she'd lost interest and was already dipping into Porky's trouser pocket, no doubt trying to extract money for a drink.

As tempting as it was to trade insults with her, I knew it would achieve nothing and regardless of what I thought of her, there was something pathetic about seeing her in such a state. You must remember how glamorous she used to be, Mark, with her hair and make-up always just so. Yet there she was looking like she needed a good wash, wearing an ill-fitting dress and

149

laddered tights. I turned to leave but she put out her arms to bar my way.

'What d'you want?' she asked. 'Money?'

I laughed. The idea of asking her for financial help was a joke. Given the state of her, it was obvious she didn't have any, but even if she had been minted, there was no chance any of it coming my way.

'I ain't got nothing,' she said, as if concealing a vast fortune.

'I don't want your money.'

She smirked at Porky who was counting out just enough change to buy another half. 'Oh, 'ark at her, Porky. She's posh!'

In the absence of friends or family, when I was living on my own with Dad, books had been my only companions. Lost in their pages, I felt safe. Liam had studied English and had boxes of paperbacks that he was more than happy to share. He'd had elocution lessons as a kid and spoke beautifully. I hated sounding like Dad and did my best to echo Liam. Sadly, Porky's estuary vowels seemed to have rubbed off on Mum.

'Stuck-up cow!' she sneered, hanging onto his arm for support.

The only good thing about the encounter was that you weren't there to see her like that, Mark. Then again, perhaps you're not the little four-year-old I imagine you as. Perhaps you've grown up. All the same, it's best if you remember her just as she was, your perfect Mummy.

'I need to talk to you, just for a moment. Please.' Under the circumstances pleading with her didn't sit well but I was desperate.

'Whatever you've gotta say, you can say in front of Porky.' She gave him a mawkish look but he was too busy lighting his cigarette to notice. He inhaled deeply before puffing out smoke rings, a trick he was clearly proud of. Mum looked at him as if he'd just performed open-heart surgery. It was all I could do not to remind her about locking me in the wardrobe. Given the state of her, I doubt she remembered. The only thing to do was catch her earlier in the day, before she was too far gone.

'Enjoy yourselves,' I said, hesitating, wondering whether to mention you but the last thing I wanted was to sully your memory. I'd tell her another time how much I loved you and how losing you had ruined my life. I wondered if she had regrets. I doubted it.

She blinked twice then stood and watched me go. Judging by her vacant expression, I could have been anyone. I pushed down the hurt feelings that had gripped me from the moment I'd seen her lurch out of the toilet and told myself it didn't matter, it didn't matter at all. The main thing was I'd found her and that meant I was one step closer to the truth. Next time, I'd be prepared, know not to expect too much and have a few tricks up my sleeve to get her to part with information. Twenty fags and a box of matches should do it.

Of course, I should have gone straight home but I couldn't bring myself to leave, not straightaway. It was frustrating. The answers were all there; I just had to ask the right questions. I went outside then hung around the bus stop, just in case she came out of the pub. I didn't have to wait long. About ten minutes later, Porky appeared, steering Mum unsteadily out through the door and along the pavement. He had his work cut out. She was weaving all over the place and I could hear her shouting, insisting she needed a wee. He kept telling her to shut up and to wait 'til she got home and demanding to know why she hadn't gone in the pub? Mum wasn't listening and before he could stop her, she'd hitched her skirt up above her thighs, yanked down her tights and peed right where she squatted. Porky let go of her hand and walked off, leaving her to hobble after him, her tights still round her ankles. Disgusting, yet pitiful. This was the woman who, when given a choice between new undies for herself or new clothes for me, picked the lacy bra every time. Mark, she may not have been up to much as a mother but she certainly knew how to turn heads on our estate.

Porky can't have gone more than a hundred yards or so when he turned down a litter-strewn path, leading to a tatty terraced house. After stabbing at the front door with his key, he eventually managed to insert it in the lock. He fell inside, closely followed by mum. He shouted and as the door slammed behind them I thought I heard her scream. My first instinct was to go and knock, bash away until someone answered, then drag her out, insisting she came home with me. Needless to say, I didn't do any of that, Mark. Without looking back, I turned and walked as fast as I could in the opposite direction, my head down, not wanting anyone to see me cry.

CHAPTER SEVENTEEN

By the time I got home, Liam had put Billie to bed and was reading him a story. It was the same one Mum used to tell you. I don't think she could read. I never saw her with a book or even a newspaper but she knew one tale, about a bear and its lost cub, off by heart. Liam doing the bear's voice, low and gruff, was the last thing I heard before I locked myself in the bathroom. I turned on the taps and let the roar of the water drown out the pain. To my surprise, Liam was outside waiting when I emerged.

'You okay?' he asked, reaching for my arm. 'Where have you been? I was worried. I thought perhaps after what I'd said, you'd...'

He hugged me. It was nothing more than a tight, ungenerous embrace and I think we were both relieved when he let go. I looked into his face to check I'd read him right. He looked washed out, so much older than the day I'd first noticed him, watching Mrs Reynolds as she ferried plates of bacon and eggs to her guests. I remember he caught me looking and turned away, embarrassed.

'Let's go and say goodnight to Billie,' he suggested, his voice a barely audible whisper. He did his best to rearrange his tired features into something resembling a smile as he led me into the nursery. I'd forgotten how good his hand felt in mine.

Poor Liam, none of it was easy for him. He'd never signed up to be a house-husband, yet there he was having to do everything. I couldn't help think my reluctance to be a mother to Billie made me less attractive to him. He didn't understand. I was sacrificing time with my baby, not because I didn't love him but because I did.

Billie was lying in his cot, on his back, breathing softly, his eyes closed. My heart jolted. He looked just like you, Mark. I let go of Liam's hand and gripped the side of the cot. I reached in and stroked your… his downy cheek.

'Don't!' said Liam, then seeing my hurt expression added. 'Sorry, I didn't mean … I just thought you might wake him.'

It was too late. The damage was done. He still didn't trust me. I'd yet to prove how I would cope without Mrs Reynolds. Trust is a weird thing, Mark. It's like a favourite toy, once you've broken it, you can try and repair it but it's never the same. Neither of us knew how to be with each other anymore.

'He's perfect,' he whispered as he turned to me. 'He's got your chin.'

I couldn't help myself. I kissed him. It was nothing more than a peck, a thank you for being kind.

'What are you doing?' he asked pulling away. 'Nothing's changed. What I said still stands. Either you sort yourself out or I go and Billie comes with me.'

The following morning, he took Billie to the park, like he often did. They were usually gone for at least two hours, plenty of time for me to visit Mum. After the last meeting, I was in no hurry to see her again, but Liam had given me no choice. I had to find out as much as I could about what had happened before you died. How closely did my memories match hers and just how envious of you was I? It wasn't something I liked to think about but Mum would be only too happy to remind me what a jealous little girl I'd been. As it was still early I figured it was unlikely she would have had a drink and was bound to be home, probably still in bed, sleeping off her hangover.

Jumpy, and if I'm honest, frightened of what I might discover, I got ready quickly and made my way back to the shabby house near the pub. It was a fifteen-minute walk at most so it was odd I'd never bumped into either her or Porky. Then again, I'd been lost in my own world for so long, Mark, I rarely noticed anyone. Even if Mum had seen me she wouldn't have recognised me. Over the years, I'd altered my appearance, so when I looked in the mirror I didn't see her staring back at me. The slightest likeness had to go. For starters, I cut and coloured my hair, dieted constantly to ensure I remained thin, almost boyish, and rarely wore make-up. What do you think, Mark? Do you like my hair? Does it suit me? Actually, that's a good point. Can you actually see me? I've always thought you could. I imagine you perched up high, not on a cloud or anything like that but in the branches of the tallest tree you can imagine, looking down, watching what we're all up to. Even if you're not, I'm convinced you know what I'm thinking and that helps, a bit.

I was so anxious about seeing Mum I'd forgotten everything I'd planned to say to her. I hesitated before going up the path and even thought about turning back. Even if she was willing to talk, the drink was bound to have warped her memory. Judging by the state of her when I'd last seen her, she was rarely sober. Nonetheless, like me, I was certain she had relived that awful day many times, going over every detail until the facts turned into fiction, creating a version of events that was easier for her to live with. We all do it, Mark. We'd go crazy if we didn't. The pain would be unbearable.

I walked up the path to the front door. Someone had taped over the plastic bell so I knocked and waited, shifting from foot to foot. When no one came, I picked my way over the filthy sweet wrappers and crushed drink cans that had blown in off the street and made my way over to the window with its chipped paintwork and rotting frames. Old sheets, hanging in place of curtains, prevented me from seeing inside. I went back to the door and rapped again. Silence. Just as I was about to give up, I heard Mum's voice.

'Who's there?'

I could see her outline, distorted through the frosted pane to the left-hand side of the door.

'It's me, Susan.'

She didn't reply straightaway and when she did she sounded less cautious, more curious. 'What d'you want?'

'I need to talk.'

'Got nuffin' to say.'

'It's important. It's about Mark.'

Just as I imagined, your name was the magic word. My heart began to thud as I heard the lock slide across. The door opened just a fraction, revealing the right-hand side of her face, one eye fixed on me. It was an odd reversal, like we'd swopped and it was her turn to be locked in the wardrobe.

'Any nonsense and I'm calling the police.'

The idea of her involving the law was laughable but I nodded all the same. I needed to see her. She opened the door, creating just enough room for me to squeeze through, and motioned me into the hallway. Before she could change her mind, I stepped inside. The place stank, a soupy mix of damp and stale smoke. Her eyes never left mine as she patted down her dressing gown pocket, her long thin hand reaching in for her cigarettes. Lifting the packet to her mouth, she flipped back the top and pulled out the last remaining cigarette with her teeth. Then, with me following, she made a beeline for the living room; the only sound the soles of her feet sticking to the linoleum as she walked.

'Get on with it, Porky'll be back soon,' she ordered, picking up her lighter from the table. Her hand shook, knocking the top off the pyramid of cigarette butts piled in the ashtray.

It was revolting. I've never smoked and can't understand why anyone would want to. Standing there, watching her inhale like she was taking in nectar, I felt no connection, nothing. I was nothing like her, was I? Surely, we couldn't be more different. I reminded myself no matter who or what she was, she had lost you, her only son. It must have affected her in unimaginable ways. Given the state of her and the house, she struck me as someone who struggled simply to exist.

'Sit down,' she said, gesturing to one end of the sofa covered with a stained orange throw. 'I'd offer you a drink but I got no milk.'

'It's fine.'

'So?' she asked, taking another drag and pursing her lips together, emphasising the lines on her upper lip.

I searched her face, desperate to discover traces of the woman I remembered, the one with the flawless skin and glossy hair. There was nothing. Even the blue eyes had faded to grey.

'Look,' I said, opening my handbag to find the small, framed photo of Billie I'd grabbed off the shelf before leaving home. I held it out to her. To my surprise, she snatched it and began tracing the outline of the baby's face with her forefinger.

157

'Oh it's Mark!' she exclaimed, as if you'd come back to life and walked into the room.

'No,' I corrected. 'He's Billie, my son.'

'That's my Mark,' she said with utter conviction, frowning as she re-examined the image.

'No, he's Billie, your grandson.'

She looked at me, then back at the picture before exhaling two thin plumes of smoke through her nostrils like a dragon.

'He don't look nuffin' like ya.' The comment sounded spiteful. I can only assume it was meant to. We both knew it wasn't true but I didn't want to argue.

'He's just like Mark, isn't he?' I said.

She handed me back the picture before looking away.

'I miss my Markie.'

I wanted to tell her I did too but before I could get the words out, she got up and hurried into the kitchen. I heard her blow her nose. I gave her a moment, then went in, watching as she took one last drag on her cigarette before flicking it into the sink and opening the fridge. It was empty but for three cans of lager, the extra strong kind, the sort that spins you into oblivion faster than any fairground ride you can imagine, Mark.

'Don't touch 'em. They're m'breakfast,' she said, grabbing one, yanking back the ring pull before putting the can to her lips. I waited for her to finish, hoping the drink would encourage her to open up but I had underestimated her tolerance for alcohol. It took all three cans to loosen her tongue. As I watched her drink them, I thought back to those days when it was the four of us at home. Nowadays, they have a name for our sort of family. 'Dysfunctional'. Funny word, isn't it, Mark? Everyone uses it: social workers, the press, even teachers. From what I've seen, it doesn't solve much; it's just an easy label to slap on people who don't quite fit the mould.

'I never had no more kids. No-one could've replaced Markie.' It would've taken a heart of stone not to feel sorry for her but I knew she'd have been more than happy to replace me. 'Not having a family never bothered Porky. He prefers his freedom, does Porky. That day, I only popped out for a minute, you know that, don't ya?'

I remember hearing her say those very same words to Dad after the accident. She didn't seem to understand it was the worst excuse she could have given.

'I'd never have gone if I'd known what would 'appen,' she went on. 'Might 'ave known I couldn't trust you.'

I knew she blamed me but I had hoped with time, she might see things differently.

'I was only little,' I said.

'You was old enough not to let him do what he did. You'd heard me tell him a million times not to touch 'em. Them pills was in the cupboard, above the sink. I kept 'em there deliberate so Mark couldn't reach 'em. Why didn't you stop him?'

Good question. Why didn't I? Or did I? Did I try to stop you, Mark? I need to know.

Mum was glaring at me. I looked down at my shoes. They were ugly, black leather lace-ups, left over from my waitressing days. I had to say something. 'It happened so quickly, one minute he was standing on the stool, the next ...'

'All I know, he was alive when I left and dead when I come back. You was in charge. He was your little brother, you should've looked out for him.'

I wanted to remind her you'd been her responsibility, hers and Dad's, not mine but I stopped myself. It felt like an excuse and a pretty flimsy one at that. Just for a moment, she looked horrified, as if the music only she could hear had stopped and she was left holding the booby prize in a macabre game of pass-the-parcel. Whatever realisation she may have had didn't last.

'Weren't my fault; I weren't there.'

Again, I didn't reply, making space for her to fill. I think it dawned on her what she thought was the perfect alibi was, in fact, an admission of guilt.

'Happy now?' she snapped, opening drawers and cupboards, no doubt on the hunt for fags or booze or both.

'No, no I'm not. How could I be? It was my fault. I've never been happy.'

'Cheer up, at least you've got your boy,' she hissed bitterly.

I didn't blame her for being jealous but I had to put her right.

'That's just it, I haven't got my son, not really.'

'What d'you mean? Where is he? You ain't left him on his own 'ave yer? The irony of the remark was lost on her.

'He's with his Dad. He's always with his Dad. I can't look after him.'

She raised her eyebrows and made that horrible face of hers, you remember, Mark. 'At least your son's alive. You should've got help for Mark. At least, come and found me. I could've saved him.'

'For the last time, I was just a kid. Even Dad didn't know what to do.'

'What d'you mean, he 'didn't know what to do'? He told me he called an ambulance and gave Mark the kiss of life.'

That was true. He had called an ambulance and he had given you the kiss of life. I struggled to remember the exact sequence of events. I could picture Dad rushing over when he saw you on the floor. Then, I think he backed off and paced around. Yes, that's right. I remember, he kept going to pick up the phone but then he'd stop and walk away.

'He did call someone eventually. I remember him shouting, really yelling. I think he'd just started to give Mark the kiss of life when the ambulance-man arrived. I remember him dragging Dad off Mark. I remember being terrified because I thought the man was attacking Dad.'

'Mark was dying for God's sake. The first thing he should've done was call a fucking ambulance.' Her face was close to mine, her features knotted into a ball of anger. 'Mark was his son. What the hell was he thinking?'

It was a good question. I just hoped Dad could give me the answer.

CHAPTER EIGHTEEN

I left Mum's house that morning, still trying to make sense of what she'd said. It was drizzling, that fine rain that soaks you right through. As I pulled back the sleeve of my cardigan to look at my watch, the face became spattered with droplets, making it difficult to read the time. It had just gone twelve; Dad would probably be starting his lunch break. I figured if I was quick, I'd just catch him. The factory was a fair walk but that suited me; I needed time to think what to say. As you know, Mark, communication never was his strong point.

I hadn't seen him since the day I'd left home. We hadn't exchanged birthday or Christmas cards and certainly hadn't celebrated Father's Day. He didn't even know I'd had a baby, or if he did I hadn't told him. As you know, Mark, we'd never been close. When I left home to live-in at the B&B he must've been delighted. I assumed he still lived at our old place, but I couldn't face going back there. I decided to visit his work. In the unlikely event of him having moved on and bothered to find another job, someone would point me in his direction.

The chat with Mum had disturbed me. Yet I couldn't, wouldn't believe Dad had deliberately left you to die. He loved you too much. I suppose he just panicked. Arriving home to find you collapsed with an empty pill bottle at your side must've blown his mind. Faced with similar circumstances,

163

we'd all like to think we'd do the right thing but who knows, Mark? In my experience, people rarely act in the way you hope. Me included. And you come to that. What in God's name got into you that day? Mum had told you a hundred times not to touch those tablets. Oh God, I'm sorry, Mark forgive me. I shouldn't blame you. It wasn't your fault. I should've done something, anything.

Suddenly, the familiar smell hit me like a sweet, sickly fog, transporting me back to when we were kids. Remember how Dad's clothes used to stink when he got home from work? Biscuits. He made biscuits. He never spoke about it but I used to overhear Mum telling him baking was for sissies. We never had much proper food in our house but weren't short of a custard-cream or two, a free box of broken biscuits every now and then being the only perk of the job. After that incident in the wardrobe, I can't look at a custard-cream now without feeling sick.

The factory was well off the main drag and not somewhere you'd ever go unless you had to. The nearer I got to the imposing iron gates the more apprehensive I became. A steady stream of workers spewed out onto the pavement, all lighting up fags like their lives depended on it.

I didn't recognise Dad at first, with his shock of grey hair, thick-rimmed glasses and baggy trousers, like a throwback from the 50's. His appearance had changed but not for the better. His eyebrows were grey. Combined with the silvery stubble and stony eyes, he looked more like someone's grandfather, than our Dad.

'Hello, Dad.'

'What the hell are you doing here?' he asked as I approached.

'I need to talk to you,' I said, the rain heavier, running down the back of my neck. I wanted to shelter somewhere but Dad was in no hurry to move. He gave off a musky odour. As he lifted his hand to rub his forehead, the sour scent of stale sweat wafted towards me. I was about to say something when he suddenly spotted a gap in the traffic and ran across the road where he disappeared into a cafe. I followed, dodging cars and just missing being hit by a bike. The cyclist skidded on the wet tarmac and shouted an obscenity at me. I felt like crying.

Still shaking, I ran into the café. It was packed with workers all clamouring to be served and make the most of their break. Dad had managed to wedge himself into a seat beside the window. I sat opposite him and found myself faced with the previous customer's dirty plate, egg-stained cutlery and a thick strip of congealed bacon rind that looked like a broken elastic band. My stomach turned. Dad noted the look of disgust on my face.

'Sorry, I'd have booked the Ritz if I'd known you was coming.'

I didn't reply. We both just sat there, neither of us looking at the other. Eventually, with much sighing, he dug his hand into his trouser pocket and pulled out a handful of coins. 'All I got 'til I get paid.'

I shrugged. 'I just need to talk to you.'

He shifted in his seat. I could tell that just me being there made him feel uncomfortable. Looking round, he beckoned the waitress over. I recognised her, she used to live down our road. You used to play with her. Oh God. You'd be the same age as her. You'd have a job too and be all grown up. Funny, how I still thought of you as a little boy. Much to my embarrassment, Dad began to flirt with the waitress. Judging by the poor girl's reaction, his lascivious comments were a regular occurrence. I looked away and heard him ask for two teas. She left, returning a few minutes later. Dad gave her a wink as she placed the drinks on the table. He watched her go as she hurried to another table. He ripped open three sachets of sugar and poured the contents into his cup. Stirring his tea noisily, he set my teeth on edge. The windows were all steamed up. A kid, a little boy a bit like you, was drawing pictures on the glass with his fingers. I leant forward and held Dad's gaze. His eyes, magnified by the thick glass lenses, were terrifying.

'It's about Mark.'

He shook his head and turned away, uttering a defiant, 'No.'

'But it's important.'

'I said, 'No'.'

Without any warning, he got up with such force he pushed the table into my stomach, winding me and spilling the tea. By the time I'd caught my breath he'd gone. I went after him because I had to know, Mark. I had to. This time, I waited impatiently for a break in the traffic before crossing the road and when I eventually caught up with him, he was already heading through the factory gates. I couldn't let him get away.

'Why didn't you call an ambulance the minute you saw Mark lying there? Why did you wait?'

I had never questioned him before. Never dared. A sudden surge of adrenalin hit me, making me feel nauseous. I looked at him, waiting for him to deny it, to assure me he'd done everything possible, that it had been a tragic accident and by the time he'd arrived there was nothing he or anyone could do. Sadly, he didn't say any of that, just stood and looked at me with those bulbous eyes, feet planted wide apart, his hands balled into fists. 'I think you've said enough.'

'Tell me,' I begged.

'You've got a nerve. I don't see yer for years, then yer show up 'ere, out the blue. What's your game?' He tried to dodge past me but I took hold of his sleeve. I don't know who was more shocked, him or me.

'Why didn't you help Mark? He was your son.'

'Mark? He didn't mean nuffin' to me,' he said, tugging his arm away then pinching his thumb and forefinger together to demonstrate just how little he thought of you. I'm sorry, Mark. I could try and hide this from you but there'd be no point. Trust me, you need to know. There's worse to come but don't put your fingers in your ears, like you used to when Mum went out. Please listen because I need to set the record straight, for you and Billie.

Dad waited until a group of men went past, all hollering and joking, before he spoke. 'You don't get it, do ya?' My insides liquefied. Even in my wildest moments, the thought had never crossed my mind but I was slowly beginning to see where this might be going. 'Keep up. He weren't mine, he was a bastard.'

'Don't say that.'

Until that day, the thought you might not be his son had never occurred to me. Apart from anything, you were the spitting image of him. Everyone said so. In my attempt to discover the truth it seemed I'd uncovered the biggest lie of the lot. I'm sorry, Mark, stay with me, just a bit longer. You need to know.

'And?' I prompted. 'But you did try to save him, yeah? Did all you could?'

You and I both knew he was hard and tough and cruel, and all the things no one wants their Dad to be but I never thought even he was capable of such evil. When he didn't reply, I swallowed the bile that rose up my throat like mercury in a thermometer.

'You can't have let him die just because you thought he wasn't yours? Surely, even you …'

'D'you really wanna know?' he interrupted, taking a step towards me; his rain-soaked coat smelt like a wet dog. He screwed up his eyes and pulled up his collar against the downpour. Water ran in rivulets down his lapels. My gut twisted. There was nothing he could say to justify what he'd done.

'That afternoon I was on me way home from work. I dunno why but I'd gone a different way back, fancied a change I suppose. Anyway, I saw yer mum coming out the pub, pissed, hair all messy, skirt halfway up her backside. She was all over some bloke. I was wild. I loved her but I'd had me suspicions for a long time. I couldn't ignore what I'd seen, couldn't let her make a monkey out of me. I wanted to frighten her, say something to make her behave her bloody self. So I told her straight. 'That's it. I'm off and I'm taking the boy with me.'

My heart jolted. Dad hadn't threatened to take me too, because Mum wouldn't care. Losing me would have no effect on her. More importantly, the threat was horribly familiar. Liam had given me the same ultimatum, almost word for word. I'd heard enough but kept listening.

'She was a crafty cow, used to tell me Mark looked like me. 'Oh, he's got your eyes,' or 'He's just like you when he smiles.' Sly bitch. Fooling me into loving him, looking after him.'

Except you didn't look after him when it mattered, did you? I thought.

'I'd have done anything for that boy, you know that. I'd never wanted kids until he come along. You was a mistake. I told her to get rid, but she was too scared.'

I winced. It was like Dad had forgotten I was a real person with feelings, let alone his daughter. I pushed down the hurt and tried to concentrate on the important bits, the bits that mattered.

'When yer Mum said she was pregnant again, the last thing I wanted was another kid. She knew that. Trouble was yer Mum weren't right; she weren't the full ticket,' he put his finger to the side of his head to indicate her unstable mental state. 'That's why she was on all them tablets.'

For the first time, it struck me the most likely reason she was unstable was because of him.

'Then Mark come along. He was a good baby, no trouble, different to you. I knew yer Mum wouldn't be bothered by me going but I thought the fear of losing Mark would make her see sense. But when I said I was off and taking him with me, she just laughed. Straight up, she laughed. Wanna know what she said?

I shook my head. I wasn't interested in him or his sordid story.

'Go on, have a guess.' He stepped even closer in that intimidating way of his. There was no one around, just the last few stragglers hurrying back to work, throwing spent cigarettes into the gutter. My right leg began to pulse. 'She said, and I remember it as clear as it were yesterday, 'You can't take Mark. You can't take him because he ain't yours to take. He's Porky's'.'

169

I gasped. It couldn't be true but even if it was it was no excuse for letting you die. Dad continued to justify himself and play the victim.

'Well, you can imagine what that done to me, can't yer? I'd brought that kid up all them years and he weren't even mine. He was that …'

'But you loved him. You don't just stop loving someone, especially not a child, do you?'

'You do when it ain't yours and its mum's been putting about.'

I was dumbfounded but I needed to know the full story and pushed on.

'So, you came home, saw Mark on the floor and did what?' I asked, still not willing to believe his actions had been as callous and deliberate as he made out.

'You know. You was there. He took them tablets long before I come in,' he said giving me a sly look from under his brow, implying your death was my fault. 'I told you to look after him 'cos I was goin' be late; I rang you from the pub.'

Of course, I remember. That day, he had called the house. Finally, there it was, the memory buried for so long. Thinking back, I can hear the distinctive ring of our phone echoing down the hallway, demanding to be answered. I didn't want to leave you, but the noise would not stop. By the time I got back to the kitchen it was too late.

My last words to you had been, 'Don't eat Mum's sweets,' before dashing to answer the phone thinking it was her calling like she always did, to check I was looking after you properly, slurring down the phone before the pips went because she'd never put enough money in. If I didn't pick up within three rings, she'd go mad and I'd be for it when she got home.

The thing is Mark, that day it wasn't Mum on the end of the line. It was Dad. He was making no sense. I kept telling him I had to go, that you needed me but he told me to shut-up and listen. Eventually, he hung up. By the time I got back you were on the floor, not moving.

It wasn't my fault. So why do I still feel this bad? I should've taken the pills off you, ignored the phone or at least told Dad I couldn't speak. Anything but left you.

When Dad spoke again, his tone had changed, his voice was softer and I could tell, he was reliving every moment. Judging by his expression, he was in hell. 'I left yer Mum outside the pub, and went to another one just round the corner. That's where I rang you from.'

'How could you have been so irresponsible? You knew Mark and I were alone in the house, two little kids, yet, you deliberately chose not to come home. If you'd done the right thing maybe you could have saved Mark. In fact, if you'd got back when you should have done, none of it would've happened, I'm convinced of that.'

He hung his head.

'Why didn't you do something as soon as you saw him on the floor?' I demanded.

He jabbed at his chest, angrier than I'd ever seen him, his voice thick with emotion, his features taut. 'When I saw that kid facedown, I didn't see Mark, I didn't see a real person, just Rawlings' bastard.'

The sense of hurt and injustice rose up inside me but before I could make my point, he started again, louder this time. I must have been soaking but I don't remember the rain, a single passer-by or even the smell of that God-awful factory. It was as if the whole world had stopped to listen to what he had to say.

171

'You was crying, begging me to help. 'Make Mark wake up, Daddy! Make him wake up.' But I couldn't go near him, couldn't bear to look at him. Then you grabbed me sleeve, screaming yer bloody head off, 'Daddy help Mark! Daddy help Mark!' You wouldn't shut up, going on and on at me, driving me to distraction.'

So, I did do something. Too late but I did try to help you. It was a relief, of sorts. Meanwhile, Dad was still making out he'd done the right thing.

'I bent down, turned him over and… it was then… I saw his face. I couldn't just let him die so I ran to the phone, called an ambulance. You remember, don't you, I called an ambulance? You was still crying and screaming so I ran back to him…did what I could but …'

He covered his face with his hands and began to howl. A couple of the factory workers pointed at us, no doubt thinking we were having a laugh, just messing around.

'Whatever Mum did or didn't do, Mark was your son and you were his Dad. Or as good as. You were all he knew. He loved you, trusted you yet you stood by and did nothing. I can't believe you let him die just to hurt Mum.'

People can be very wicked, Mark. Often those closest to home inflict the worst damage. Dad trying to justify his actions just made it worse. When people know they are in the wrong, they over-explain, tell you what they did and why they did it, going on and on. If only they could hear themselves.

'Years later, after she'd cleared off for good with that arse-hole, I discovered the slag had been going with him for years. I found all his letters; she'd kept 'em in a box, underneath the bed, my fucking bed. The dates all added up. The kid was his alright.'

'But you couldn't know that, not for sure?'

He sneered then walked away, turning down through the gates without looking back. I called after him but he just kept walking, Mark. I felt so empty, a thousand memories blew through me in a moment and I watched as you flew away and seemed to fade to a point where I couldn't see you, not even your face. It was like losing you all over again.

I had to keep going because all this delving about in the dust was as much about Billie as it was about you. Trouble was, I already knew too much. What was I supposed to do? Tell the police? Tell Mum? Tell myself it didn't matter anymore and leave the past where it belonged? No, I couldn't do any of that, Mark, because if there's one thing I do know, I'm not my father's daughter.

CHAPTER NINETEEN

Obviously Dad's confession, if that's what you can call such a crass admission, rocked me to the core, the horror eclipsing any sense of relief I might have felt at discovering I was not to blame for what happened to you. Obviously, I was relieved, Mark. I'd blamed myself my whole life and can't help thinking I could've done more. Finding out Dad deliberately let you die is beyond my understanding. That's the trouble, Mark, we search for the truth in the hope it will make everything right, but often, when we find it, we often wish we hadn't.

I had to tell someone about Dad and had no intention of keeping his awful secret. My first thought was to talk to Liam but since he was considering leaving me, discovering my Dad had all but killed his own son would hardly persuade him to reconsider. Apart from you, there was only one other person I could trust, Mrs Reynolds. Given her condition, it was likely to be a one-sided conversation but she would listen and that would be enough. Besides, I owed her a visit. With everything that had gone on, I had neglected her.

The next morning, I was in turmoil with it all. Luckily, Liam didn't ask too many questions about where I'd been the day before or why I was late home. Somehow I managed to keep it all together and even helped Liam get Billie ready. It was odd given the circumstances but I felt more relaxed and able to cope. Since Dad's revelation, the nagging doubt I was not fit to be a mother had been silenced and my love for Billie, previously locked away, burst out of my heart like a shriek of joy. With his head nestled against my shoulder, my beautiful son was where he belonged, in my arms. Anxious to make up for lost time, I treasured every moment. 'I love you, Billie-Boy,' I whispered, kissing him on the top of his head.

Liam was pleased to see me taking an interest; he kept grinning and giving me sidelong glances. I took it as a sign of hope. At last, he was willing to give me some space to just be with Billie. The three of us left the house looking like any other family. No one seeing us that morning, with me proudly pushing the pram, Liam by my side, would have guessed the horrific back story. That's often the way, Mark. Most of us keep our true selves hidden and present as near perfect a front as we can to the world. We walked into town where I bought the biggest bunch of flowers I could find.

'Who are they for?' Liam asked.

'Mrs Reynolds. I'm going to pop in and see her on the way home. You take Billie back. I promise I won't be long.'

For some reason I couldn't fathom, Liam was desperate to come with me, which struck me as odd given he didn't really like Dot. More importantly, if he came I wouldn't be able to tell her about Dad. Just as I was struggling to think of what to say to deter him, Billie obligingly threw up. It was his party trick and always timed to perfection. I could see he was fine. Like a cat having a fur-ball, he looked much brighter afterwards but couldn't show up at Mrs Reynolds' covered in vomit, leaving Liam no option but to take him home.

When I arrived at the B&B, I had no idea what to expect. Strokes affect people differently, Mark. Some recover relatively quickly but others take longer and suffer terrible side effects.

'Oh it's you,' said Dot's sister, Deirdre. She opened the door wide to show off the immaculate hallway. 'I suppose you'd better come in. Here, I'll take those.' She snatched the bouquet from me, accidentally knocking the stems against the side of the door, causing the chrysanthemums to shed a few petals onto the pristine floor. Tutting loudly, she bent down and picked them up. I sneezed. 'Not ill, are you? I can't have Dot getting sick. I've got to get back to my business ... been here too long as it is ... can't have her exposed to germs. I say, can't have her exposed to germs.' Her Scottish accent was out of place. I always expected her to sound just like Dot.

'I'm not contagious, just allergic to pollen.'

'We haven't seen you for ages and that was weeks ago. Dot's missed you. I say, Dot's missed you.'

I could feel my face colour. She looked at me as if waiting for an explanation.

'I've been busy ... with the baby.'

It wasn't a total lie. All this raking over the ashes of the past, uncovering long-buried secrets was as much for Billie's benefit as yours. Once your death was finally resolved and those to blame were called to account, I could be a proper Mum to Billie.

'We've had a bit of a breakthrough ... not out of the woods by a long chalk ... not by a long chalk,' she said ushering me along the corridor. 'The doctors say her recovery is down to me. Well, I have been with her day and night but that's what families do. Have you got brothers or sisters, Susan?'

A normal enough question yet not one I'd been asked in a while. 'Er, yes, I have ... had ... a brother. He ... he died.'

She stared at me, shocked, as if not knowing what to say.

'It was a long time ago,' I added, trying to make her feel less awkward.

She smiled gratefully and for the first time, I could see a real resemblance to Dot. Without another word, she showed me into the back room where Mrs Reynolds was sitting in an armchair watching television. I prayed she'd be up to hearing what I had to say.

'Let's turn that rubbish off, shall we? You've got a guest. It's Susan, you remember Susan?' She snatched up the remote from the table and pressed the button. The screen went blank. 'That's better. We can all hear ourselves think now. I say, we can all hear ourselves think.'

Dot looked distressed but when she turned and saw me, her face brightened.

'Hello, Dot, how are you?' I asked, taking her hand, so much thinner than the last time I'd held it, the papery, transparent skin displaying a web of blue veins.

'Better,' she said in a voice I didn't recognise.

Just that one word was an effort. Seeing her, I couldn't imagine telling her about Dad. The shock would be too much for her.

'Told you we've turned a corner,' said her sister smugly.

'Flowers, for you, Dot,' I told her pointing to the bunch in Deirdre's arms.

'Better get them in some water ... see if I can revive them. They look half dead,' she declared leaving the room and not a moment too soon. I just wanted my time with Mrs Reynolds.

'Alright then, Dot?'

She nodded and I was pleased to see a light in her eyes I'd never noticed before. Whatever it was, I was sure it wasn't down to her sister's constant companionship or me showing up unannounced. No, there was something else making her shine.

'Oh I've got something for you, Dot.' I let go of her hand and reached into my bag for the picture of Billie, the one I'd taken to show Mum. 'Look, how he's grown.'

She ran the tip of her forefinger over the picture and beamed. It was wonderful to see her so happy, Mark. She opened her mouth but before she could say anything, her sister bustled back in. My heart sank.

'What you got there? Oh, I recognise that baby,' she said peering at the picture. 'His Dad brought him in to see you, didn't he?'

There had to be some mistake. After all, they say one baby looks much like any other. More to the point, why would Liam go out of his way to visit without telling me? No wonder he was so insistent on coming with me. Dot's hands fluttered to her face.

'When was he here?' I asked.

'Tuesday morning. I remember because I was on my way to a hair appointment. Dot had the telly on full blast and I almost didn't hear the knock, I say I almost didn't hear…'

'What did he look like?' I interrupted.

'Well, you should know. I take it this is your baby?' she asked, pointing at the photo. 'He was good-looking, very well spoken. He came twice, first on his own, then with the baby.'

'Was Dot okay with it?'

'She was. I wasn't. I had no idea who he was. The first time, he insisted on talking to Dot in private. I refused but she got agitated so I let him stay and listened at the door, just in case. I couldn't hear a thing; he was whispering. He didn't stay long.'

'And how was Dot after he left?' I asked.

'Excited. She was thrilled when he showed up again with the baby. That time, I made sure to leave the door ajar so I could see what was going on. My heart was in my mouth when he handed her the baby. I thought she'd drop the wee thing but she sat there looking as pleased as punch.'

'I don't get it.'

'He's your boyfriend, ask him.'

I looked at Dot but she was too busy studying Billie's photo to notice. Liam's visit made no sense at the time, Mark. Like many things in life, it was only later that everything fell into place.

'Could I please have a coffee?' I asked, any excuse to get rid of the woman for five minutes so I could talk to Dot alone. Deirdre looked a bit put out but left the room.

'Well … done,' croaked Mrs Reynolds once she was certain her sister was out of earshot.

Mark, the last thing I wanted to do was upset her but I had to ask. 'Dot, what did Liam want? I need to know.'

She took a deep breath and for a moment, I thought she was going to cry. I was just about to call for help, when she spoke, each word clearly an effort.

'Wanted…to…show…me… Billie.'

'But you know Billie. You used to look after him. Remember?'

Her face clouded. Then, she looked at the picture again and it was as if the sun had come out.

'I'm his … nan.'

'Billie's your grandson?'

Sometimes I can be very slow on the uptake but eventually I got it. It was obvious. Liam was adopted. Mrs

Reynolds was his Mum. His real Mum. His birth mother. No wonder he went to the B&B. It wasn't me he was interested in, it was Dot. She reached out to squeeze my hand. I gave her a kiss. Her cheek smelt of violets. Her lop-sided smile said it all.

'Ah, I knew it!' said her sister reappearing in the doorway, a mug in one hand. 'No wonder you cleared off to London when you did, Dorothy. After you went, Dad wouldn't have your name mentioned in the house. Was it that boy you used to go with, the smart one from the college? I bet it was.'

Mrs Reynolds didn't answer. She didn't have to. It was obvious from her expression her sister was right. I had no idea who this man was but Dot didn't suffer fools, and Billie's grandad sounded like a bright spark. I was delighted my son was descended from two special people. I hugged her, a little too enthusiastically but I couldn't help myself. It was a wonderful surprise to discover the woman who had been a surrogate mother to me was my son's grandmother.

All the same, I couldn't help wondering why Liam hadn't told me all this himself. At first, I was annoyed. Surely, he should have wanted to share it with me? Then again, his behaviour was nothing unusual. Ever since I've known him, he's kept everything inside, making it impossible to know what he's really thinking. Even the ultimatum, about leaving me and taking Billie with him, had come out of the blue. I had no idea he was unhappy enough to want to leave. Fancy not letting on he'd been to see Dot. I wonder how long he'd known she was his Mum.

That said, I hadn't been much of a partner and even less of a mother. I was too wrapped up with what had happened to you to think about anything else.

181

I still hadn't mentioned Dad to Dot. She'd know what to say. I had to tread carefully, the last thing I wanted to do was upset her and ruin her newfound happiness but now she was family, this was her business. She needed to know.

As calmly as I could, I recounted the whole sorry tale, telling her what Dad had told me about believing you were Porky's son and leaving you to die. When I'd finished, I was drained. She remained calm. Older people are often like that, Mark. That generation must have experienced so much during the war, they're unshockable.

'Please, Dot, I don't know what to do for the best,' I said anxiously waiting for her to reply.

When she finally spoke, I was stunned by her suggestion.

'Tell … your … Mum.'

At first I was horrified at telling her what I'd discovered but you were her son, she deserved to know the truth. I still couldn't quite get my head round the fact that she was as much to blame as he was. She made some terrible mistakes that day.

Dot handed Billie's photo back to me.

'Keep it,' I told her. 'It's yours.'

She put it on the table, propped up against the clock, in pride of place where it belonged. Deirdre may have taken credit for her recovery but I knew differently. Things had changed; Dot was no longer on her own. She had a son and a grandson to get well for.

As I left the house, I saw Liam walking towards me with Billie, all clean and changed, in the pram. It must have been obvious by the look on my face I knew his secret.

'I'm sorry, Susan. I wanted to tell you but it was never a good time.'

'I can't believe you've known all along that she was your Mum yet you never said a thing. How could you keep something that big from me? What does it say about us?'

He folded his arms across his chest. His face was grey. 'I'd been looking for her for ages, long before I met you. When I finally traced her to the B&B I turned up to confront her about why she'd abandoned me when I was just two days old. Two days? Can you imagine leaving Billie at that age?'

It sounded like a dig at me but I don't think it was meant.

'Then, when I saw her, I couldn't do it. I couldn't go in there all guns blazing so I decided to sit back and get to know her from a distance.'

'You mean you spied on her.'

'No, not at all. You don't know what it's like. You're not adopted. I had to tread carefully. For all I knew, she might have had a family, husband, kids; people who didn't even know I existed. I couldn't go barging in. It wouldn't have been fair on anyone but having found her, I had to know more. I started going to the B&B for dinner, just once or twice to begin with but by the time you joined, I was a regular customer. It was nice, comforting, having her cook for me after all those years.'

'So how long has Dot known?'

'Not long. I told her after her stroke, I had to.'

'How did she take it?'

'You know her better than I do. How d'you think she took it? She was thrilled, said she knew I'd find her one day. The trouble is, Susan, I'm still angry with her for giving me up.'

Then the penny dropped, Mark. Finally, it all made sense. 'So that's why you were so rude to her? And why you didn't want to let her look after Billie?'

183

He nodded. 'She rejected me. I wasn't going to give her the chance to do the same to my son.'

'You should've said something then. Not kept it all to yourself.'

'Susan, don't do this. It's not fair. We both know it wasn't a good time.'

'I don't get you. Why did you wait so long to look for her when you'd known all your life that you were adopted?'

'I loved my Mum. My real Mum, the woman who brought me up, loved me all her life. She died a couple of years ago and I got depressed. I was in a terrible state. I had no other family to help and I couldn't cope. I went to see my GP and he referred me to a counsellor. I felt so alone, it just felt like the right time to find Dot.'

I nodded. It made sense. 'So, how are you feeling now? It must be good to finally have your Mum in your life?'

'I told you. She's not my Mum. My Mum's dead,' he snapped.

'Okay, I'm sorry. Just give Dot a chance. She'd not had it easy. Please don't be too hard on her.'

I kissed his cheek and put my arms around him. He returned the hug. It felt good. Slowly, we walked home together through the park. 'So Dot never guessed the gentleman on table three, watching her every move was actually her son?'

'No, it's strange. You'd imagine Mums would instinctively know when they were close to their offspring.' He grinned at me. It was good to see him relax a little.

'She must've been over the moon, especially about Billie being her grandson?'

'Yes, delighted.'

'Thank God for that. He's given her a reason to live. She needs us, Liam. Her sister's not going to hang around here much longer. She's done her stint.'

'No way. We're not looking after her. We've got enough to do with Billie.' He stopped and stared at me, his eyes cold.

'Yes, but...'

'No! She didn't look after me. Why should I look after her?'

It was a childish, petulant response. Yes, he was upset but Dot was ill and I had no intention of abandoning her. 'She did what she thought was right at the time, Liam, just like we all do.'

He didn't respond. Just walked on, pushing the pram, in that slow, steady way of his. He was in shock. I was sure he would come round eventually and his relationship with Dot would work itself out.

It was different with Dad, Mark. Given what he'd told me, there was no hope of a happy ending.

CHAPTER TWENTY

'Mum, it's me,' I shouted through the letterbox after I'd given up knocking.

'What d'you want?' she asked, eventually opening the door, her unmade-up face emerging from a cloud of cigarette smoke.

'Can I come in?'

'No, Porky's in bed.'

'Please, it's important.'

She glanced over her shoulder, then reached up and took her coat off the hook.

'Go to the pub. I'll be five minutes.'

I made my way back down the street to the place where I'd first seen her and Porky Rawlings. The barman eyed me knowingly, I guess he recognised me from the time before. 'She'll be in soon, for her white wine.'

I bought two glasses and took them over to a corner table where I sat and waited, toying with the beer mat on the table, flipping it through my fingers. I was nervous, Mark. What I'd discovered had been a sickening shock, to think I'd been living with Dad all those years after what he did without even knowing. True to her word, Mum arrived a few minutes later. She had applied some red lipstick, over-emphasising her pale skin and giving her a ghoulish appearance. She sat down, immediately picking up her glass.

'Thanks,' she murmured licking her lips.

'How have you been?'

'How have I been? You're not interested in me. What's up?'

She was right; the last thing I wanted to do was make polite conversation.

'It's about Mark.'

It was always about you. As ever, she came alive at the mention of your name but I could see the memory was bittersweet. Like me, she'd never got over losing you. I understood her pain. It was hard for me losing my brother but no parent should outlive their child. It goes against the natural order of things. If that parent feels they are somehow to blame in whatever way, their suffering must be racked up to unbearable proportions. No wonder Mum drank so much. I couldn't afford to get sidetracked. I had to talk to her before Porky turned up.

'I went to see Dad.'

She raised her pencilled-on eyebrows at me. I took a sip of wine. It tasted like sulphur.

'You should've said, I'd have come too. We could've had a party.' She drained her glass and set it down on the table waiting for me to refill it.

I couldn't just blurt out what Dad had told me. I had no idea how much she knew. Perhaps he'd told her everything and that was the real reason she'd left. Then again, if she'd known, surely she would've told the police? After all he had killed her son, but she was on shaky ground having left two young children alone in the house. I'd say she was equally to blame.

As you know, Mark, Mum was unpredictable. It was best to tread carefully. I needed to sound her out carefully before telling her what Dad had said about thinking you were Porky's son. According to her, she and Porky didn't have kids. But we both know she was a good liar. She had to be; she'd had an affair for years.

'You and Porky, I was just wondering...'

'Spit it out.'

I nodded to the barman, who had already poured another glass of wine in readiness. He brought it over and I gave him the money, telling him to have one himself. The more Mum drank, the looser her tongue became. She polished off the second glass in record time. Perhaps she was as nervous as I was. She was looking round the pub, no doubt looking for someone to cadge a cigarette off. I didn't want her to get distracted and jumped straight in.

'Did you have any more children?'

'I told you before. No. What's all this about anyway?' Her tone was suspicious. It was easy to underestimate her in her addled state.

'So I don't I have any half-brothers and sisters I should know about?'

She laughed. 'If you do they ain't mine. Porky can't have kids.'

'What?' Please God, this was even worse than I'd imagined.

'Porky can't have kids. He's a Jaffa! Seedless!' She laughed at the age-old joke. I thought I was going to be sick.

'What? Has that been the case ever since you've known him?'

'Oh yeah, he's always fired blanks,' she said, laughing. She must've mistaken my horrified expression for something else because she continued to snigger. 'Whatever you do, don't tell him I told you. He likes to think he's all man.'

She stared at my drink. I gave her the wine. I didn't want it. I felt too ill.

'And you only ever went with Porky. No-one else?'

'You cheeky cow. Are you calling me a slag?'

'No,' I said quickly, desperate not to get on the wrong side of her. At least not before she'd answered my question. 'No, of course not. I just wondered if you had other boyfriends before Porky?'

'What d'you take me for?'

She had no idea why I was asking or what I was getting at. She had no reason to lie to me.

At long last, this was the truth, revealed in all its ugliness. Dad had killed his own child and Mum was as much to blame.

'So why did you lie and tell Dad that Mark wasn't his son? Why did you say he was Porky's?'

'Because, I knew yer Dad meant what he'd said; he would've left and taken Mark with him. I had to lie to keep Mark. I knew there was no way yer Dad would've looked after another man's kid.'

She looked pleased with herself, like she'd somehow done a good thing. I couldn't believe it. Between the pair of them, they had as good as killed you. They were responsible.

I was so angry and lost no time in explaining that the reason why Dad had delayed getting help for you was because he had believed her and thought you were Porky's son. It was no excuse and did not diminish his crime but at least I knew why he'd done what he'd done. I might have known Mum was to blame. Not that she had any intention of facing up to her part. 'The bloody murderer. I'll have him. I swear to God, I'm going kill him.'

I let her rant on, not listening, not wanting to hear her pass the buck. Although not directly responsible, Mum was hardly the innocent victim in all this. Had she stayed faithful to Dad, he would have had no reason to think you weren't his. And, if she hadn't left us alone that day, you might still be here.

Regardless of Mum's shortcomings, Dad was guilty of a crime even worse than I had imagined. That day he had allowed jealousy, anger and ego to get the better of him. All these years, he had let me believe it was my fault, giving a seven year old child an unbearable burden.

Mum was still screaming and shouting and calling Dad a 'murdering bastard' when I left the pub. I didn't stop running until I reached our old house. When I got there I could hardly breathe. My throat was burning, my heart hammering. I banged on the door with my fists, causing shards of green paint to flake and reveal the old black paint beneath.

When Dad didn't answer, I flicked open the letter box and peered in. It was a Saturday; he wouldn't be at work. I was sure he was there. I could see steam rising from a pan on the hob.

'Open the door or I'll just stand here shouting until you do.'

Within moments, he appeared looking tired and dishevelled from the front room. I let the letter box snap shut and waited. He opened the door. Seeing him again, face to face, I found it hard to breathe.

'We need to talk,' I said pushing past him into the hall.

'What's your game, coming round 'ere shouting the odds?'

I ignored him and went straight through to the kitchen. It was much shabbier than I remembered and much smaller. It stank of boiled cabbage. I looked around and in that instant a hundred memories were revived. There was the sink and the cupboard where Mum had kept her pills. The small, square mirror in the door was cracked, reflecting and distorting. Suddenly, Dad pushed past me to tend to the pan boiling over on the stove. He grabbed it and flung it into the sink.

'Soddit! You've ruined me dinner.'

He sat down on a stool. I wanted to kick it from under him. It was the same stool you had clambered on to reach the sink that afternoon. I could see the red crayon mark I'd made on the side.

'Mark was your son,' I said looking him straight in the eye, something I had never dared do as a child.

'Don't start all that again. I told yer, he was nuffin to me. He was Porky Rawlings' bastard.'

'You're wrong. Mark was your son. Porky can't have kids, Mum told me.'

'You're lying.' The colour drained from Dad's face, his mouth slackened.

'I'm not like you. Why would I lie? Mark was your son. You only had to look at him to see that, a Wheeler, through and through.' I took out the photo of you. The little black and white one I'd always carried with me and thrust it in his face. He turned away, not wanting to look. Not wanting to see.

'Nah.' The raised vein in his temple throbbed underneath the taut, tense skin.

'Yes, look at him. He was your son and you let him die because you didn't think he was.'

He leapt up and ran upstairs. I heard a door slam. He'd have to come out sooner or later and when he did, I'd be waiting. I glanced down at the floor. Even the linoleum was the same. I could still see it, covered with what looked like yellow polka dots, Mum's tablets. And, there in the middle, was you, face down, not moving. I could even picture the yellowing crepe soles of the red leather sandals you were wearing and the way your hair was shorn into a perfect little 'V' at the nape of your neck.

The sound of the loo flushing startled me. I looked up and the clock caught my eye. It had just gone two. I opened a cupboard and took out a tin, lifting the lid on a pile of broken biscuits. The smell made me feel sick so I replaced the lid quickly and put the tin back on the shelf. Next to it was your old feeding cup - you remember, the blue one with the two handles, one on either side? Fancy him keeping that. I could picture you in the kitchen, sitting on the floor, pulling all the pots and pans out and grinning up at me, so pleased with yourself. I glanced back at the clock. He'd been gone over fifteen minutes, a long time even for him.

'Dad!' I called. 'Dad!'

No reply. I ran to the foot of the stairs and looked up. The bathroom door was still shut. I raced up the steps, two at a time. I knocked on the door. No answer. No, I wasn't going to let the bastard take the easy way out.

'Dad!' I screamed trying the handle. 'Open the door!'

When we were kids, I remember, the little silver bolt on the inside of the toilet door was held on by just two screws. It never looked very secure and I worried someone would burst

193

in on me. Like everything else in the house, it was bound to be the same one, Dad never having bothered to repair or replace it.

I called twice before shouldering the door. Two goes was all it took for the lock to give way. The door flung open and there was Dad on the floor, slumped against the wall, a half-drunk glass of water by his side.

'What have you done? What have you taken?' I asked picking up a handful of opened pill packs from the side of the bath.

He was still conscious but his eyes were flickering. 'What you doing?' he murmured.

'What you should've done all those years ago, you bastard,' I replied, running downstairs and into the hall. I picked up the receiver and dialled '999'. When the operator asked what services I required, Mark, I didn't hesitate, I knew exactly what to say.

'Ambulance. And police.'

Running a B&B had never been my ambition but now with Liam doing the books and Dot overseeing, it's a lot more fulfilling than being a waitress. Once we've finished serving breakfast, I usually help get Dot and Billie ready and Liam takes them off for the rest of the morning. Provided it's not raining, they all like the park. Billie loves messing about in the sandpit and Dot keeps a watchful eye. I told you Liam would come round, didn't I, Mark? He's quite close to his mum now. Although, he still insists on calling her Dot. She says she doesn't mind but I'm not so sure. At least, she's 'Nana' to Billie. Sometimes, we all go together but Liam likes it when it's just the three of them. I understand. They need their time, need to make up for all those lost years.

I like living here. The guests make a fuss of Billie and I get to spend every day with him when he's not being monopolised by his Nana. Cooking never was my strong point so I leave all that to Liam and stick to what I know, cleaning the rooms and serving the customers. Liam reckons we'll soon be doing well enough to hire some part-time staff, giving me more time with Billie. I can't wait.

I never see Mum. Our paths don't cross, I make sure of that. I can only imagine she's still propping up the bar, a white wine in one hand, a fag in the other, Jaffa by her side.

And as for Dad, he made a full recovery after the overdose but you'll be pleased to know he won't be baking any more biscuits anytime soon, unless it's in the prison kitchen. Apparently, he was so riddled with guilt, when he realised what he'd done, he made a full confession.

Liam and I are getting on well, a little too well perhaps. I am pregnant, a boy, due any day now. You can guess what I'm going to call him, can't you, Mark?

After all these years of torment, we finally know the truth. As much as I'd love to turn back that clock in the kitchen and bring you back, I can't. We always knew this was never going to end happily for you but at least you're in no doubt I loved you then like I love you now.

That's it. I've said all I need to say. Thanks for listening and helping me to make sense of the past for all our sakes. You know I have to go, don't you? Billie needs me and I just felt the baby kick. I promise not to disturb you again. Rest in peace, Mark.

THE END

Thanks for reading this book. If you enjoyed it, a short review on Amazon would be appreciated.

Please keep in touch. I'd love to know what you think of the work. Stop by **www.joan-ellis.com** and follow me on twitter @joansusanellis

Disclaimer: All persons are fictitious.

By the same author:

Psychological Thriller

The Killing of Mummy's Boy.

'I slit someone's throat,' the man told the woman on the 4.20 from Waterloo to Portsmouth. It was Sandra's first journey back to London since she had moved to the Isle of Wight a few years before. Having a stretch of water between her and the mainland made her feel safe. The Solent could be expensive to cross; some people thought twice before making the journey. She liked that.'

Two strangers. One shared interest. Murder. Ben slit a man's throat. When Sandra discovers she's being stalked, she turns to the least likely person for help, with terrifying consequences.

'Terrifying'

☆ ☆ ☆ ☆ ☆

Trish Jackson

'Don't read alone'

☆☆☆☆☆

Lee Cradock

'Gripping. A real page turner'

☆☆☆☆☆

Mary G

'I couldn't put this book down. It was impossible to guess the identity of the stalker, and the author did a wonderful job of projecting Sandra's terror, her protectiveness toward her son, and the emotional turmoil she experienced when she realised she was attracted to Ben.'

Trish Jackson. Author

☆☆☆☆☆

'Weirdly, I could put this book down. I had to. I didn't want to finish it too quickly. I wanted to savour its surprising twists and turns. I wanted to appreciate the very human strengths, weaknesses and foibles of its protagonist and the taut, tantalising plot. In the end, of course, I couldn't put it down and stayed up till 2am to find out what happened. If you're picking it up for the first time, you have been warned.'

Paul Burke. Author.

☆☆☆☆☆

'Well-written, fun read.'

Belinda, Girls Love To Read

☆ ☆ ☆ ☆

'I lost a day because of this book. I had to finish it'

Lady Roberts

☆ ☆ ☆ ☆ ☆

'I absolutely LOVED Ella David. She made me laugh endlessly. There was a smart wit about her. Ella was the sort of woman that I'd love to sit across from in an office. I'd be endlessly entertained! The characters were superbly developed.'

Becca's Books

'The writing style was humorous, serious and heart-breaking. With feelings and a good moral compass Ella could be a role model for women.

The Bookshelf

'I am Ella Buy me.' is one of the sharpest and wittiest books I have read. Ella is a brilliant lead character.'

Bookaholic Confessions

☆ ☆ ☆ ☆

Coming soon: Autobiography

The Things You Missed While You Were Away

'*Being paired with a chair at the local National Childbirth Trust anti-natal classes did nothing for my ego. Unlike the other mums who were with their husbands, the only arms supporting me through the breathing exercises were wooden ones.*

My daughter's childhood in the 90s was very different to my upbringing in the 60s. As neither of us knew what it was like to have our Dads at home, the book is written as a letter to my Father highlighting the moments he never got to share. It is for anyone who has been a child, if only to prove when we lose someone special, love comes from unexpected places to fill the space in our heart.